The **Year** of the **Rat**

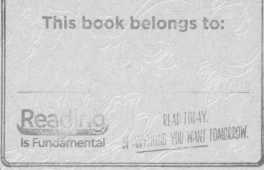

This book belongs to:

_____

The Year of the Rat

A novel by

Grace Lin

LITTLE, BROWN AND COMPANY
New York   Boston

Text and illustrations copyright © 2008 by Grace Lin

Cover photo of girl © SensorSpot/Getty Images; photo of boy © Ryouchin/Getty Images. Cover design by Liz Casal. Cover © 2019 Hachette Book Group, Inc.

Little, Brown and Company
Hachette Book Group
1290 Avenue of the Americas, New York, NY 10104
Visit us at LBYR.com

Originally published in hardcover and ebook by Little, Brown and Company in January 2008
Paperback Reissue Edition: March 2019

Little, Brown and Company is a division of Hachette Book Group, Inc.
The Little, Brown name and logo are trademarks of Hachette Book Group, Inc.

The publisher is not responsible for websites (or their content) that are not owned by the publisher.

The Library of Congress has cataloged the hardcover edition as follows:

Lin, Grace.
The year of the rat / by Grace Lin. —1st ed.
    p. cm.
Sequel to: The year of the dog.
Summary: In the Chinese Year of the Rat, a young Taiwanese American girl faces many challenges: her best friend moves to California and a new boy comes to her school, she must find the courage to forge ahead with her dream of becoming a writer and illustrator, and she must learn to find the beauty in change.
ISBN-13: 978-0-316-11426-4 (hc) / 978-0-316-03361-9 (pb)
1. Taiwanese Americans—New York (State)—Juvenile fiction. [1. Taiwanese Americans—Fiction. 2. Chinese New Year—Fiction. 3. Schools—Fiction. 4. Identity—Fiction. 5. Family life—New York (State)—Fiction. 6. New York (State)—Fiction.] I. Title.
PZ7.L644Yer 2007
[Fic]—dc22

2007012327

ISBNs: 978-0-316-53134-4 (pbk.), 978-0-316-02928-5 (ebook)

Printed in the United States of America

LSC-C

10 9 8 7 6 5 4 3 2 1

If you are reading this book,
it is dedicated to you.

My Family during
the Year of the Rat

Chapter 1

The **Year** of the **Rat**

glasses of wine
and cups of juice

"HAPPY YEAR OF THE RAT!" DAD SAID AS HE toasted us with his glass. The clinking noises filled the air as the adults knocked glasses of wine against the kids' cups of juice.

It was the eve of Chinese New Year, and my best friend, Melody, and her family had come for the celebration dinner just as they had for the last two years. Before Melody moved to upstate New York, I always celebrated Chinese New Year with just my family—me, Ki-Ki, Lissy, Mom, and Dad—because we were the only Asian people in the area. But since Melody and her family were also Taiwanese, they came to celebrate the New Year with us.

As usual, the table was covered with food. Mom had to make enough food for ten people (Melody also had five people in her family—two brothers and her parents) and leftovers. There always has to be food left over after a Chinese New Year dinner because that means you'll have more than enough for the year. So the platters of pork, yellow

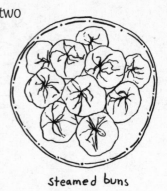

Steamed buns

noodles, roasted duck, soft cotton-white steamed buns, fried dumplings, delicate silver fish, and vegetables so shiny they looked polished, crowded the table. There was barely enough room for our plates.

"Ugh, Year of the Rat," Lissy said at the dinner table. "I liked last year better, when it was the Year of the Pig. I was lucky then."

I rolled my eyes at Melody. She just gave me a small smile. I could tell that since her parents were here and they were guests for dinner, she had to be polite. She couldn't make any rude faces like she normally would with me.

But since it was my house, I didn't have to be polite.

"Oink! Oink!" I snorted. "Lissy's a PIG!"

"Pacy," Mom said in a way that meant "behave."

"You're not supposed to say anything rude or bad on the New Year," Melody's mom said. "Or you'll bring bad things into the year."

Well, that bothered me. I didn't want a whole year of bad luck just because I said a couple of silly things. I quickly quieted down.

"In America," Dad said, ignoring me, "rats are looked down on. But Chinese people actually admire rats."

"Why?" Benji, Melody's younger brother, asked.

"They think the rat is very smart and charming," Daddy said. "And he's first."

"What do you mean, first?" Ki-Ki asked.

"You know the story of why all the Chinese years are named after animals, right?" Mom said.

Lissy and Felix nodded, but Ki-Ki shook her head. "I remember a little," I said. "But I forget."

"Okay, I'll tell you again," Dad said.

THE STORY OF THE TWELVE ANIMALS OF CHINESE NEW YEAR OR HOW THE RAT WAS FIRST

A long time ago, so long that you couldn't even imagine it, the Jade Emperor had a birthday. Since he was the Jade

3

Emperor, the king of all the heavens, he invited the animals on the earth to come to his celebration. And, he said, to add to the festivities, it would be a race. The first twelve to arrive would win the prize of a year named after them.

So, of course all the animals wanted this honor. But separating the earth and the Jade Emperor's palace was a large and forceful river, with violent waves that rose and crashed over and over again like the pounding of a thunderous drum. All the animals worried about getting across.

Many animals decided to train and prepare themselves for the event, like athletes before a marathon. One such animal was the cat. Every day he worked—strengthening his muscles, holding his breath, and trying to get used to water. The night before the race, the cat put himself through vigorous exercises one last time. Exhausted, he went to bed, asking his friend the rat to wake him up in the morning in time to start the race.

The rat agreed, but his mind was elsewhere. The rat knew he was a poor swimmer, too weak and too small to manage the river's waves. But he wanted to be an honored animal. He refused to give up. So, all night he sat and thought and plotted.

Rat and water buffalo
cross the river

In the morning, the rat followed the strong water ox like a shadow. As soon as the race started, the rat made a flying leap onto the ox's back. The rat was so small and light that the muscular ox didn't even notice he was there. And, since the water ox was the best swimmer he was easily leading the race. The powerful ox had no fear of the rough water he wallowed in everyday. Even with the fierce waves fighting him, he moved forward undaunted.

But, as soon as the Jade Emperor's kingdom was within range, the rat gave another flying leap and was the first ashore. He was the winner! So, the rat was rewarded by having the first year named after him.

The ox was second. And then the tiger, then the rabbit (who had made it across by jumping from one river stone to the next), the flying dragon (who wasn't first because he stopped to make it rain for some people), the snake (who had wrapped himself around the horse's ankle and scared the horse when he slithered off, causing the horse to jump back), the horse, then the sheep, monkey and rooster (who had built a raft together), the dog, and then lastly the pig (who was late because he got hungry on the way and stopped to eat). And so, the twelve years were named.

And what about the cat? The rat forgot to wake him up in the morning, so he slept through the entire contest. That is why there is no Year of the Cat. That is also why whenever a cat sees a rat it hisses and attacks. The cat has never forgiven the rat for not waking him up and making him miss the race.

Cat hisses at Rat

"So, the rat was the first of the twelve animals to finish the race," Dad finished. "That's why his year is first."

"So that means Lissy has to wait twelve whole years before it's her year again!" I said. I knew I shouldn't, but I couldn't resist annoying her. "Ha-ha!"

"Yes," Mom said as she nodded. "And, you know, since the Year of the Rat is the first year of the next twelve-year cycle, it symbolizes new beginnings."

"And that means changes," Melody's mom said, and she gave her family a funny look I didn't understand. "The Year of the Rat is the time to make a fresh start and to change things."

Melody and I looked at each other. She had a weird look on her face. I felt confused. Changes? I liked the way things were right now. What was going to happen in the Year of the Rat?

almost the
New Year

THIS YEAR, CHINESE NEW YEAR WAS ON A Saturday, so we could stay up late. After dinner, we all gathered in the family room. As Dad made a warm fire in our fireplace, Ki-Ki almost closed her eyes from sleepiness.

"Uh-oh," Lissy said. "Wake up, Ki-Ki! You have to welcome in the New Year!"

"Yes," Melody's dad said. "We have to keep you up all night. The longer you stay awake, the longer lives we will have."

"Then you better do something to keep us awake," Melody said. "Do something so we're not bored."

"Oh, you want us to entertain you, huh?" Dad laughed. "Okay, let's see. I can sing. Do-re-mi . . ."

"NO!" we all said together.

"How about if you all write down your New Year's resolutions?" Dad said. "You can think about what you want to accomplish in the New Year."

"You're supposed to do that for the American New Year," Lissy objected. "Not Chinese New Year."

"So?" Dad said. "We celebrate both. We can make up our own traditions."

Even though it seemed a little bit like school, it didn't sound so bad. So, I got paper and pencils for everyone. When we sat down and started to write, I grinned at Melody. I knew that the one thing that both of us really wanted for the New Year was for Sam Mercer to like us. He was the cutest boy in our grade. But neither one of us was going to write that down!

Pacy's Resolutions

1. Write and draw another book, like I did before, and be an author and illustrator

2. See and ride a unicorn, though a white horse would be okay, too

3. Have lots of money and be rich

4. Become famous

5. Have good luck in EVERYTHING

9

When Mom and Dad read my resolutions, they laughed.

"Well, these are very unusual resolutions," Dad said, "though I guess most people would like to share your last resolution."

"Americans write resolutions," Mom said. "Chinese and Taiwanese people write wishes. I think some of the things on your list are more like wishes."

"Is there a big difference?" I asked.

"Well, a resolution is something you can try to accomplish," Mom said. "For a wish to come true, it needs someone else to make it happen."

"Resolutions are better," Dad said. "You're more powerful. You don't have to depend on anyone. A wish is left to fate, but a resolution is a change you make yourself. You can change your destiny with your resolution."

I didn't really understand what Dad was talking about—fate and destiny and resolutions? I did like the idea of being powerful, but I also really liked the idea of someone else making my wishes come true—that seemed a lot easier. I looked at Melody's list. Hers were a lot like mine, except for one.

Melody's Resolutions

1. Read 100 Books
2. Get Good Grades
3. Win the Lottery
4. Be the Luckiest Person in the World
5. Stay in New Hartford

"Why did you write 'stay in New Hartford'?" I asked. New Hartford was the name of our town, the one we lived in now.

Melody looked sad. "I wasn't supposed to tell you because we aren't supposed to have sad feelings on New Year," she said. "But my mom told me we might be moving."

"Moving!" I said. "You can't move! You just got here."

"I know," she said. "I don't want to. But my Dad's company wants to give him a job in California."

"California is on the other side of the country!" I said. "That's too far. You can't go."

"Well, my mom said maybe," Melody said. "So, maybe we won't. Let's hope for good luck."

"Pacy, Melody!" Mom said, calling us over. "It's almost midnight." Mom

party hat and noisemaker

handed us funny hats and noisemakers, and we all watched the clock. But, even though I blew and yelled when the clock hit twelve, I was quiet and worried on the inside. Melody was my best friend—we did everything together. If she left, I would be the only Asian student in my elementary school, except for Ki-Ki. If Melody moved, everything would change.

Chapter 3

Rats

my haversack

MELODY AND I BOTH WENT TO THE OXFORD Road Elementary School. Our teacher, Ms. Magon, was very strict about talking in class. She made Melody sit on the right side of the room and me on the left side, because she said we talked too much when we sat next to each other.

But on the Monday after Chinese New Year, we weren't sitting in the classroom. We were going on a field trip! Our class had been studying about the American Revolution and so everyone in our grade was going to a place called Fort Stanwix. It was a real fort that the soldiers had used during the war. We were all going to pretend that we were American soldiers and experience what it would have been like there during the Revolutionary War.

Our class had been preparing for this trip for a long time. We had to sew our own *haversacks*, which were the bags that the soldiers carried all their things in. I wasn't happy with my haversack. Mom had given me an old pillowcase to make mine out of, so it had buttercup flowers sprinkled all over it. I thought it was ridiculous. What soldier would have a yellow, flowered haversack?

How to make a Haversack

1. fold fabric so there is extra on top
2. Sew sides
3. Sew strap to back with "x" Stitches
4. Sew button on front
5. fold flap over and cut slit for button

We were going to eat like soldiers, too; we were going to make homemade stew over a fire. So everyone was assigned to bring an ingredient. I brought a turnip, while Melody brought an onion. She was kind of worried about the onion because at the grocery store it was labeled a "Spanish Onion" and we didn't think the Revolutionary soldiers would get onions from Spain.

turnip

14

Spanish Onion

But Ms. Magon said it was okay.

Before we went, Ms. Magon divided us into ranks. There was going to be a sergeant, two corporals, and two cooks from each class. The rest of us would be privates. Ms. Magon picked the names from a bowl. Melody was a corporal! I didn't get picked, so that meant I was a private.

Since Melody was a corporal, she had to walk at the front of the line when Ms. Magon gave us our "marching orders" to the bus. I walked in the back with my other friends Becky and Charlotte. They were fun. Becky was the one who named Melody and me "The Almost Twins" because we had so many things in common—like being the only Asians in school. Becky had curly brown hair, while Charlotte had pale waves like unbraided silk rope. Before Melody had moved here, they had been my best friends. We were still friends now, but Melody was my best friend.

marching with Becky and Charlotte

"One, two, three," Becky whispered to me. "Forward, March!"

"This is so silly," Charlotte said. "Revolutionary War soldiers wouldn't be getting on school buses."

"Yes," I said. "But if we were Revolutionary War soldiers, we'd have to march all the way there."

"And stay there," Becky added. "We'd have to eat there and sleep there in the dirt with rats! Yuck!"

"Rats aren't that bad," I said, thinking about the Year of the Rat and Dad's story.

"What?!" Becky said. Both she and Charlotte looked at me as if I were crazy. "Rats are disgusting!"

"No," I said, trying to explain. "It's the Year of the Rat this year. And to Chinese people, rats aren't that bad."

"Ew!" Charlotte said. "Well, I'm glad I'm not Chinese then!"

I was embarrassed after that. I wished I had just kept quiet. It was so hard to explain these things. Sometimes, I felt like I was more than one person. At home, everyone called me Pacy, my Chinese name; and at school, everyone called me Grace, my American name. And it was even more confusing because I wasn't even sure if I was Chinese. My parents came from Taiwan, which (because of some adult politics I didn't really understand) some people thought was a part of China. So, some people called us Chinese while other people called us Taiwanese. At times I wasn't sure which person I was supposed to be—Taiwanese Pacy or Chinese Pacy or American Grace.

So I was glad when I saw Melody on the bus saving me a seat. Just seeing her wide grin and waving hand filled me with a comfortable, safe feeling, like opening up an umbrella in the rain. I knew she would understand. What would I do if Melody left?

Melody waiting for me on the bus

Chapter 4

Fort Stanwix

FROM THE OUTSIDE, FORT STANWIX LOOKED LIKE
a huge, old wooden porcupine—it was made out of
weathered gray-brown wood, with
pointed logs sticking out of it. It was
strange to see our bright yellow
school buses parked in front of it;
somehow it made the fort look even
older and paler.

As we got off the bus and got in
our ranks (Melody had to go to the
front again), a man dressed in a revolutionary uniform came out.

"Welcome, new soldiers," he said

First Sergeant

to us, his words making misty clouds in the winter air. "I'm your First Sergeant, in charge of your regiment. You have come to join our fight for independence from the British. While your days may be hard here, remember what we are fighting for. Remember how Britain treats us like dogs, trying to force us to pay their taxes and house them. We must fight them and be free. Give us liberty or give us death!"

I looked at Becky and Charlotte. I wasn't sure if we were supposed to cheer when he said that. The First Sergeant kept talking to us as if the Revolutionary War were happening right then and we really were newly enlisted soldiers. It was a little weird, but kind of fun, too.

drum

The First Sergeant told us that a drum would beat before all our orders. There was a drumbeat for everything—getting up, marching, and retreating. And there was an extra special drumbeat for going to battle. That one was really important to remember, because the enemy could come at any time.

Then the First Sergeant marched us around Fort Stanwix and showed us the different areas. It was good that we marched so much, because it was cold! I could feel the frosted air through my many layers, and the wind seemed to prick my face as if needles were being thrown at me. I was glad when the drum beat for lunch.

We went to the barracks for our stew. The rough ceiling was low and the sleeping area was a platform near the ground, covered with coarse straw. And the stew didn't taste good either. It wasn't like any kind of stew I had eaten before. It was kind of like soupy

stew

cooked meat-water with hard vegetables. The only thing I liked about it was that it was warm.

"Yuck," Melody said as she made a face at her stew. "Poor soldiers. They had a hard life."

I nodded, but I couldn't help thinking about the hard life I would have if Melody moved. I pushed my stew under the sleeping platform and drew a rat in the cold dirt with a stick.

"Have your parents decided if you're going to move to California?" I asked.

"They don't know yet," Melody said. "My father's company wants to send him to California for a big promotion and transfer someone from their office in China here. They'd even pay for us to move, and the Chinese family would rent our house."

"Someone else would live in your house?" I said, horrified.

"I know," Melody said as she chewed the stew meat fiercely. "Can you believe it? Someone else living in MY house, someone else living in MY room!"

"It's like the Redcoats forcing the colonists to house them!" I said. "The enemy would be taking over your house."

"Yeah," Melody said, scowling at her stew. "I hope the enemy stays far, far away."

I hoped so, too. Because deep down, when I thought about facing the Year of the Rat without Melody, my heart beat like the drum call of the First Sergeant. I just hoped it wasn't the drumbeat that warned that the enemy was coming.

Chapter 5

Max

I HAD BEEN SO WORRIED ABOUT MELODY moving, that I forgot that we were going to Albany for my cousin Max's birthday. He was turning one year old. Albany was far away, but not so far that I got to miss school. Two years ago we had gone to my Cousin Albert's birthday party in New Jersey and got to miss two days of school. Since Cousin Max lived closer, we were only going to be away for the weekend.

But even though Max didn't live that far away, it was nighttime when we got to his house. Actually, I don't remember getting to his house because I fell asleep in the car. When I woke up in the morning, I was in bed and the sunlight was streaming through the windows,

Ki-Ki and Lissy
sleeping

casting a lace pattern shadow of branches on my face and pillow. Lissy and Ki-Ki were beside me, snoring a musical duet. But it wasn't their snores that woke me up, it was the doorbell ringing. I poked my head out of the room and heard the footsteps of a crowd of people answering the door.

"Kim!" I heard Uncle Leo say. "Ja-ba, bei?"

Ja-ba, bei means "Have you eaten yet?" in Taiwanese. But it also means "Good to see you!" and that meant people were arriving for Max's party already! I went back to the room and shook Ki-Ki and Lissy awake.

"Wake up," I told them. "Max's party started already. They're starting the party without us!"

And as we scrambled downstairs, we saw all our relatives. Everyone was there—Uncle Leo, Aunt Judy,

Clifford, the
last time we
saw him

two-year-old Albert . . . The house felt like a bulging bag of uncooked rice about to burst. Even Cousin Clifford was there! Cousin Clifford was our favorite cousin. He was older than us, but not a real adult yet. We hadn't seen him in a long time. The last time I saw him, he was graduating from college with a black robe, a funny hat, and a big smile with sparkling eyes. Now, he looked pretty much the same, except not in a black robe.

"Did you start the party without us?" Ki-Ki demanded.

"No," Mom said, and laughed. "We were just getting everything ready. Look, even Max was waiting for you—he's just coming out now."

When Auntie Sue brought Max out of his room and everyone clapped and some of us yelled, "Happy Birthday!" Max smiled, and his round face reminded me of a ripe peach—soft and pink and fuzzy. He was so cute, I couldn't help going up to him and hugging him. He felt squashy and lumpy, like a pillow full of soft sand.

Max wobbled, with his arms out like a mummy, and his shoes thudded on the ground with each step. His shoes were funny. Grandma had sent them from Taiwan. They were bright green, the color of moss in the sun, with big eyes and pointed ears embroidered on them with red, yellow, blue, and white thread.

"Max has cat shoes!" I said.

"They're not cat shoes," Mom corrected me. "They're tiger shoes."

"But he wasn't born in the Year of the Tiger," I said. "I was. Did Grandma get mixed up?"

"No," Mom said. "Tigers are lucky for children. They protect them. The tigers on Max's shoes are to protect him from hurting himself while he walks. That's also why the tigers' eyes are so big—so they can look out for trouble."

"I don't think they're help-ing," I said as I watched Max stumble over the edge of the rug.

tiger shoes

"You don't know," Mom said, smiling. "He might be doing a lot worse if he didn't have them."

"Since I was born in the Year of the Tiger, does that mean I'm lucky for myself?" I asked.

"Hmm," Mom said. "Tigers are lucky for little children. I think you are too old now for tiger luck. I think, instead, you are lucky for Max. You are probably a very good babysitter."

I liked being a good babysitter. I held Max's hands as he took one uneasy step after another, and he smiled at me as I walked him from room to room. When he was tired, I read him books and drew pictures with him. I wanted to make sure I kept practicing for my own books. Max liked the drawing, though all he did was scribble.

But the whole time I couldn't stop thinking about my own tiger luck. If tigers were only lucky for little children, did that mean that every year I got older, I would get unluckier? When did I stop being lucky? When did it all change?

Chapter 6

Destiny

Long-life noodles

"HAPPY BIRTHDAY TO YOU, " AUNTIE SUE SANG AS we finished eating our lunch. We had eaten pink and brown cold meats, dried jellyfish that looked like pieces of unraveled yellow rope, a thick white soup with black specks of pepper floating in it, a whole chicken roasted chestnut brown, vegetables that looked like they had been dipped in syrup, glazed shrimp, and shining noodles. The noodles were extra long because they were long-life birthday noodles— the longer they were the longer the life they symbolized. I ate a lot of those noodles. I wasn't sure if that meant I'd have a long life, but I suspected I'd have a fat one. I was completely full!

But I did have room for dessert. Auntie Sue was

bringing in the cake; its frosting was smooth and white. Pink frosted roses, the color of a strawberry milk shake, decorated the four corners; and a single

Max's Cake

candle with a flickering orange flame stuck out from the center.

We all began singing, except for Uncle Phil, who was busy stopping Max from grabbing one of the frosted flowers. I was glad Uncle Phil didn't let Max destroy the cake, even though it was his birthday—I wanted one of those flowers.

While the cake was being served and eaten, everyone started clapping and laughing.

"What's going on?" Ki-Ki asked.

"The fun is starting," Clifford told her. "Uncle Leo has taken out the destiny plate."

The destiny plate was the shiny black and red cover of an old tray. The actual plate wasn't important; it was what we put on it that was used for fortune-telling. This was supposed to predict what Max's job was going to be in the future. We'd put all kinds of

the destiny tray

different things on the tray, and whatever he chose would tell us what he'd be when he grew up. We all watched with jokes and laughter as Uncle Leo held up the tray.

"What should we put on the tray?" he asked, his face wrinkled in a smile. "What do we want Max to be when he grows up?"

Uncle Leo collected items from everyone. Each thing symbolized a different job. He put a book on the tray, to signify a teacher. He eagerly borrowed Uncle Shin's stethoscope, to represent a doctor. He put a toy truck on the tray, to stand for a mechanic; a paint-brush for an artist; and money for a businessman. He made Aunt Kim choose the shiniest coins in her pocketbook.

"I want them to catch Max's eye," he laughed. "He can be our family millionaire."

Even arranging the items was a big joke.

"Put the stethoscope closer to him," Uncle Shin called out. "We want another doctor!"

"Move that paintbrush to the edge," Dad said.

"We don't want him to choose the cold door!"

"What does that mean, the 'cold door'?" I asked. I was a little bothered because I had already decided that I was going to be a writer and an artist when I grew up, and now Dad was saying he didn't want Max to be one.

"When they say you choose the cold door, it means you are choosing the harder life," Clifford explained. "The idea is that there are many doors you can choose to walk through—all being different kinds of lives. A lot of people think if you choose to become an artist, you are choosing a harder life—poor and shivering. You know how they always say 'starving artists'? So, being an artist is a cold door."

I didn't like that. I pictured myself opening a freezer door and being forced inside. It didn't seem that nice. Was that my destiny?

"What are you so worried about?" Clifford said.

"I want to be an artist," I told him. "But I don't want to walk through the cold door."

"Well, you have a long time to decide. I wouldn't worry about it; a lot of things can change before you have to choose," Clifford said, then he grinned at me. "Besides, any cold door you walk through is sure to be warmer than upstate New York in the winter."

I laughed, even though I was still worried. But I tried not to think about it because Max's tray was finally ready. Every carefully chosen item finally had a place everyone agreed on. Now, it was up to Max.

Auntie Sue wiped Max's hands with a clean napkin. She had let him grab the flowers off his own piece of cake, so his face was covered with pink and white frosting. We all watched as she moved Max's plate and put the destiny tray in front of him.

Max, however, was watching his half-eaten cake. He let out a bawl, ignored everything on the destiny tray, and reached out for his cake! Everyone laughed.

"Let him have the cake," Uncle Phil told Auntie Sue. "Then, maybe he will take something off the tray."

So, Auntie Sue let Max have his cake back, which he quickly smashed onto his face. As he finished demolishing it, he looked in confusion at all of us staring at him.

"Pick something from the tray," Auntie Sue encouraged

Max chooses his destiny

him, tapping the tray so that the items clinked. With one chubby hand full of cake, Max reached out and grabbed . . . the stethoscope! A big cheer went up in the room.

"A doctor!" Uncle Leo said. "Max will be a doctor!"

"I don't believe it," I told Clifford. "Max didn't really choose the stethoscope first. He chose the cake first. Maybe he'll be a baker."

"Hmm, maybe," Clifford said. "But we're going to have to wait a long time before we know who's right."

Chapter 7

Clifford's Destiny

clifford makes a speech

"SPEAKING OF DESTINY," CLIFFORD ANNOUNCED as everyone was finishing their cake. "I have something I want to tell you all."

Everyone stopped eating and looked up. This was a change. Clifford never made speeches before.

"Well," Clifford said, taking a deep breath, "you know how I have been working in Taiwan since I graduated from college? Well, I met a girl there and I've asked her to marry me, and she said yes!"

After that, no one could hear anything. Everyone roared with questions and laughter. "Is she pretty?" "What does she do?" "Where is she now?" "Where are you going to get married?" Clifford had to hold his hand up like a teacher to make everyone listen to him.

"Her name is Lian," Clifford said. "Right now she is in Taiwan, but she is coming here next week."

Congratulating Clifford

"When are you going to get married? Lissy asked.

"We're hoping this summer," Clifford said. "After your school is over so that everyone can come. I want everyone to meet her."

"Did you get her a diamond ring?" Ki-Ki asked.

"Yes, of course," Clifford said. "A big one. So much that now I am poor and don't know where we can afford to get married."

diamond ring

"Get married at our house!" I yelled. "Then I can be a bridesmaid."

Clifford just laughed as he was swallowed up by hugs from Aunt Kim and Auntie Sue. But I wasn't joking; I really wanted to be a bridesmaid. Then I could get a fancy dress and a bouquet. I never had a real bouquet before. That was something I wouldn't have minded changing in the Year of the Rat.

my school

WHEN I WENT TO SCHOOL ON MONDAY AND saw Melody, I knew she had bad news. Her face looked like it did when we lost the science fair.

"My parents said we're going to move," she told me. "My dad says it's too good an opportunity to pass up."

"All of you have to go?" I asked stupidly. I felt as if the ice-cold drops of a melting icicle were dripping on me.

"Yes," Melody said. "The enemy is coming to take over our house in two months."

Oxford Rd Elementary New Hartford, NY Report Card					
Teacher: Ms. Magon Rm 301	Student: Melody Ling 67 Laurel Rd New Hartford, NY				
	1	2	3	4	FINAL
Math	A	B+	B+	I	—
Science	A-	A	B+	I	—
History	A-	A	A-	I	—
English	A+	B-	A-	I	—
Gym	B+	A	B+	I	—
Art	A-	B	B+	I	—
Music	B	A	A-	I	—

Melody's Incomplete Report card

Melody
Kicking dirt

"Two months! That's too soon!" I said. "You'll miss everything—the last class project, your report card! You can't go!"

"I know," Melody said, kicking the dirt with her feet. "But my parents said some things can't be helped. My dad has to be there when the job starts."

"I can't believe it," I said. "Maybe my parents can talk to your parents. Maybe they could get them to change their minds."

"Okay!" Melody said hopefully.

"I know my parents could talk to them," I said, and the more I thought about it the more sure I was. "The Year of the Rat is about changes, so maybe it's about changing their minds too!"

But when I talked to Mom and Dad about it at dinner, they didn't say anything I wanted them to say.

"If Melody's parents want to move," Mom said, "it's their business. We will miss them, but we can't tell them what to do."

"Why not?" I asked. My frustration bubbled inside of me like boiling soup.

"Why can't you talk to her parents? I don't want Melody to move!"

"Pacy," Mom said, "calm down. Just because Melody is moving doesn't mean you can't stay friends with her."

"It's not fair," I said. "Can't we do anything to change things?"

"Remember what Melody's mom said about the Year of the Rat," Mom said. "It's the time for new beginnings and changes."

"I hate the Year of the Rat," I said. "And Melody resolved to stay in New Hartford. One of her resolutions is already broken."

"Ah, well," Dad said. "You have to be resigned to your fate. It looks like moving to California is Melody's fate. And no resolution can fight that."

packing Melody's books

AFTER THAT EVERYTHING SEEMED TO CHANGE.
Melody couldn't come over as much anymore because she had to pack up her stuff. When I went over
to her house, everything was in boxes. One weekend, while Dad played golf and Lissy went to the mall,
Mom, Ki-Ki, and I went over to Melody's house to help
them pack. Mrs. Pan and Sandy Pan came over to
help, too. The Pans were another Taiwanese family
that we knew; Sandy was Ki-Ki's friend. They lived in
Syracuse, which was an hour away from New Hartford, so we didn't see them that often. If Melody
hadn't been moving, packing would've been fun.

Ki-Ki, Sandy, Benji, and Felix packed the family
room, where all the toys were, and Mom, Mrs. Pan,

and Melody's mom packed the living room. Melody and I packed the things in her room. Before we started packing, I told Melody about what my dad said about artists and the cold door.

"So does the cold door mean being poor?" Melody asked.

"I think so," I said. "Clifford said it was the harder life, that artists are starving."

"But, you don't exactly want to be an artist," Melody said. "You want to make the pictures in books. That can't be the same."

"You think so?" I asked, not convinced.

"Well, if you're that worried about it you can change your mind," Melody said. "It is the Year of the Rat; maybe this is the year you change what you want to be."

But I didn't want to change that; being an author and illustrator was the one thing I was sure of. Or at least I thought so. Now, I was starting to doubt it.

"Are you two packing up there?" Melody's mom called. "Make sure you work and talk, not just talk!"

Melody and I looked at each other guiltily. "Yes!" Melody called back as I giggled. "We've filled lots of boxes!"

"Don't fill them all with your books," Melody's mom

said. "You have too many. Give Pacy some of your books, maybe half."

I was kind of excited when I heard that. Melody and I both loved books, and she had a lot of good ones. I liked getting half of them. It was easy for me to choose the books that I wanted. It wasn't so easy for Melody, though.

"Can I take this one?" I said, pointing at one book.

"No, I love that one," Melody said. "Pick a different one."

"Okay, how about this one?" I said.

"No, I love that one too," she said. "Pick another."

"This one?" I said.

"No," she said, "not that one. I really love that one."

"You love ALL of them!" I said. "There's none for me to take!"

We both began to laugh. Then we stopped because we both felt sad.

"I don't want to give up my books," Melody said. And I felt like I wouldn't have minded buying my own copies of all of Melody's books if it meant she wouldn't have to move.

"I know," I said. "We'll share them. I'll take half now

and after I'm done reading them, I'll mail them back to you."

"That's a good idea!" Melody said. "We'll share all of them. That way they'll be something we own together. And if we keep sending them, it'll be like there's something of me here all the time and something of you in California. They'll make sure we don't forget about each other."

"Yeah!" I said, excited. "That'd be fun, and when I read the books, I'll know they've been in California and I can imagine what they've seen."

"And the books I get will remind me of New Hartford," Melody said. "Which ones should go where first, do you think?"

We both looked at the big pile. There were so many books; I didn't know how we would be able to choose.

"Why don't we just close our eyes and point?" Melody said. "We'll take turns."

So, that was how we divided Melody's books. It was still hard for her, though, especially when I got the

Melody chooses her books

The Cheerleaders Books

Cheerleaders books first. We both loved the Cheerleaders books, even though our moms tried really hard to stop us from reading them. They thought the books were too old for us because they were about high school, boys, and cheerleading. But we didn't read them for any of those reasons; we read them because one of the cheerleaders was Chinese.

"That's the one where Hope wears velvet cranberry-colored pants to a party," Melody told me as I stacked one of the books into my pile. "It's the one that made me ask my Mom to get me those red fuzzy pants, so I could get an outfit just like Hope. So you HAVE to mail that to me later."

"Okay," I promised, as we brought down her boxes. "After a month I'll mail them to you and after another month, you mail the books to me again."

Melody's fuzzy pants

"That doesn't sound like a very practical plan," Mom said, overhearing our conversation.

42

"Melody can just buy copies of the books in California, instead of paying for mailing again and again."

"But it's not the same," I told Mom. "If Melody buys new copies, they won't be OUR books."

Mom shook her head and shrugged her shoulders at Melody's mom. I could tell neither one of them understood.

Chapter 10

Lunch

vegetables cooking in plain water

"I'M GOING TO MAKE LUNCH," MELODY'S MOM SAID. "We'll eat and then we can finish packing afterward."

I made a face at Ki-Ki. We didn't like Melody's mom's cooking. She always cooked dry brown rice and color-less vegetables that you had to chew a lot. She said her food was very "healthy" but we thought it was very tasteless. Even Dad joked about it. "When I eat over at Melody's house, I eat like a horse," he said. "Because Melody's mom makes me eat grass!"

Today's lunch wasn't going to be any different. I watched as Melody's mom dumped brown rice grains into the rice cooker and prepared the vegetables in plain water. The water was just starting to bubble when Felix came into the room.

"Mom," Felix said, "we need more boxes."

"We ran out so soon?" Melody's mom said. "And we still have so much to pack! I better get some more later."

"Why don't you go get some more now?" Mom said. "We'll finish the lunch and it'll be ready by the time you get back."

"Oh, good idea," Melody's mom said. "It's almost done; the vegetables just need to steam for another couple minutes."

As soon as the door shut behind Melody's mom, Mrs. Pan and Mom looked at each other.

"Kuai yi dian!" Mrs. Pan said. "Quickly, before she comes back!"

They raced to the kitchen.

"I'll brown the garlic," Mom said, grabbing the oil. "Let's hurry!"

"Yes," Mrs. Pan said, taking out the salt, soy sauce, and oyster sauce. "I'll add the

Mom and Mrs. Pan
fix lunch

45

seasoning. Quickly, quickly!"

The rest of us laughed as we watched them cook the lunch with very unhealthy ingredients.

unhealthy
ingredients

By the time Melody's mom came back, the lunch was all done. Mom and Mrs. Pan had everything on the table, and we were all sitting and waiting. Melody's mom came into the house and smelled the roasted garlic and oil and wrinkled her nose, but didn't say anything.

Mom and Mrs. Pan tried to look very innocent as they served the stir-fried vegetables and fried rice. Melody's mom didn't say a word. She just sat down at her place and started eating. We all watched her take her first bite.

"Hmm," she said, "pretty good."

And then everyone burst into laughter.

Chapter 11

Resigned to Fate

Melody and Me
in art class

EVEN THOUGH MELODY'S CLOTHES AND BOOKS
and toys were packed away and the movers had been
scheduled, it was hard being resigned to her fate.
Winter softened into spring, and the cold, icy water
dripped from our roof like a string of pearls. Every
day we counted seemed to slip by, until finally it was
Melody's last day of school.

On her last day, we had art class, and Mr. Valente,
our art teacher, finally gave each of us the special
paper to use for our poem quilt square. Everyone was
writing a poem and drawing a picture on the paper,
and afterward, somehow (I think using the computer),
Mr. Valente was going to take all the paper squares

and make them into cloth squares. Then he was going to sew all the cloth squares together to make our class quilt. We'd hang it in the classroom for the rest of the year, and after that it would hang in the cafeteria in remembrance of us.

I thought it was a little funny that Mr. Valente was going to sew the quilt. I always thought quilts were sewn by old people with gray hair and glasses like the women we read about in the Revolutionary War. Mr. Valente had big shoulders like a football player and a fuzzy mustache that looked like a brown caterpillar. I didn't think he looked like someone who

Mr. Valente sews our quilt

should sew a quilt. Melody didn't agree.

"Grandmothers and old ladies make quilts as blankets," she said. "Our quilt is going to be art. So, anyone can sew that—especially an art teacher!"

Melody wrote the best poem ever for her quilt square. I wished I could write a poem as good as hers.

Her square looked like this:

As I was waiting for the bus
the rain came down on me
Without an umbrella, there I was,
it rained so hard I couldn't see.

BUS
STOP

Melody Ling

Melody's quilt square

Mine looked like this:

I wish I was a star
That could shoot very far
And everyone could see
In the night sky,
me.

Grace Lin

My quilt square

I kind of copied how Melody rhymed "see" and "me," but no one seemed to notice. Anyway, the project was taking a long time. It seemed like we had been working on the quilt squares for weeks and weeks. Ms. Magon made us fix our poems many times and Mr. Valente made us do two practice rounds before he finally gave us the special paper for the quilt.

"I'm not going to be able to finish my quilt square," Melody said. Her face wrinkled and I could see her eyes shine with unhappiness. "Everyone else is going to keep working on the squares next week, but I won't be here."

"You can probably take it with you," I said, though I felt like my words left stones in my throat. It was hard to think that Melody wouldn't be there next week.

"No," Melody said. "If I take it with me, then I won't be a part of the quilt. And when they hang the quilt in the classroom and in the cafeteria, my square won't be in it. I won't be part of the class remembrance, and everyone will forget about me. It'd be like I never existed here!"

I hadn't thought about that. What were we going to do?

"Is there a problem, ladies?" Mr. Valente asked as he stopped by our table.

"Melody's not going to be able to finish her square by the end of class today," I told him. "And she's moving this weekend."

"Oh dear," Mr. Valente said. "Going to California, right?"

"Can I come in at recess and finish my square?" Melody asked in one breath. "I'll even stay after school to finish it. Please?"

"Yes, can she?" I pleaded with her. "Please? Please?"

"Yes, yes," Mr. Valente said. "Of course you can work on your square at recess. If you don't finish, you can bring it home and work on it this weekend before you leave, and Grace can bring it in on Monday."

After he said that, we were so happy and relieved that we felt like we had just won a prize. Melody grinned and I clapped my hands. Mr. Valente looked at us and shook his head. "You two," he said. "What are you going to do without each other?"

all packed for movers

ALL TOO SOON, MELODY'S LAST DAY OF SCHOOL
ended. During recess, when Melody went to work on
her quilt, Ms. Magon had all of us in class sign our
names and write messages in a big good-bye card. And
at the end of the day, Ms. Magon gave her the card and

Melody's bouquet and
good-bye card

a bouquet of carnations. They
were white with pink edges, and
all bunched together, the blossoms looked like ribbon candy.
Melody gave me some of the
flowers and we both wore them
in our hair on the way home.

And that weekend the movers

came and took every-
thing away, and Melody and
her family got ready to get
on an airplane to California.

Me and Melody with
flowers in our hair

We drove them to the
airport. They had so many
things that Mom and Dad
had to use both cars to
bring them. Melody and her
mother drove with Mom and me, while the rest of
her family drove with Dad.

"You'll keep in touch, right?" Melody said. "You'll
call all the time, right? You won't forget about me,
will you? Promise?"

"No, I won't forget," I said. "I promise. I'll add it to
my New Year's resolutions."

"Good," Melody said. "I'll add not to forget about
you to my resolutions, too."

movers taking
away Melody's
things

"Anyway, I have our
books," I said. "Those will
make sure I don't forget."

"Yeah," Melody said. "If
we keep sending the

Melody waves good-bye

books, it'll almost be like we're reading them together."

"Almost," I said. But as I watched her wave good-bye in the airport, I knew it wouldn't be the same as if we were together. It wouldn't even be almost the same. Everything would be different now.

"Are you sad Melody's gone?" Mom asked as we drove back from the airport.

I shrugged. I didn't want to say anything. I could feel the tears burning in my eyes, and I was afraid if I said anything they'd start falling. And I was too old to cry just because a friend moved away.

"It's okay to cry," Mom said. "I know you'll miss her."

"I'm not crying," I said crossly, wishing Mom didn't

always know everything. "I'm not a baby."

"Crying because you miss someone doesn't have anything to do with how old you are," Mom said. "When I left Taiwan, Amah cried so much that my sisters and I still talk about it."

"Really?" I said. Even though I felt miserable, I was curious. "She must have cried a lot."

AMAH WATERS THE ROSES

My Amah—your great grandmother—and I were very close. I was her first grandchild, so she spent a lot of time with me. She walked me to school every day, fed me and washed my clothes. When we had fish for dinner, she would save me the eyes (the best part), like glittering diamonds, to eat. Even when I grew older, I was her favorite. Whenever she won at mahjong, she would secretly beckon me to her room and give me a special treat of candy-covered berries or tea-colored cakes filled with soft, sweet bean paste. And when I decided that I wanted to grow flowers she encouraged me, even though everyone else thought it was a waste of time.

"It's a lot of work to take care of plants," my parents said. "Make sure you don't neglect your studying."

"Wouldn't you rather go out and do fun things," my sisters and brother asked, "than spend all your time taking care of plants?"

"Why don't you grow some roses?" Amah said, slipping me some money. "I know you like those the best."

Now, our house in Taiwan was an apartment building, a cardboard-colored rectangle with many levels. Cement surrounded the house, and instead of trees, buildings shadowed us. And instead of blades of grass, people and cars and signs crowded the ground.

So, since there was no place for me to grow anything around the house, I grew my flowers on the roof. I

Mom plants roses

balanced pots in my arms and dragged bags of soil up the stairs. Every day, I watered and dug and planted. And in the summer, when everything was in full bloom, Amah would come up and admire the flowers.

When I left Taiwan to come to the United States, I was sad to leave my garden. Even though my brother and sisters said they would take care of it, I knew it was not important to them and they would soon forget.

But I hadn't considered Amah's devotion. My departure was heartbreaking for her. Whenever she saw an old shoe or a book I left behind, she would weep. And when she saw my siblings ignoring my garden, she decided to take care of it for me.

So even though Amah's feet had been bound—the horrible and painful old tradition of deforming a girl's feet to make them small—she climbed four flights of stairs to water and prune my gar- den. Her arms shook as she carried the pails of water, and her tiny, throbbing feet burned as red as the bright- est rose. But those were small

Amah
(Mom's
grandmother)
Climbs the
Stairs

concerns to her. She cared for each plant, lovingly brushing the leaves and patting the soil. Sometimes as she poured water into their pots, she would remember our happy times together, and tears would fall from her face.

When I came back that summer to visit, Amah was so happy to see me.

"I took care of your garden," she told me. "Come and see."

And I was stunned. The roof seemed to be blazing with flowers. The blossoms were larger and brighter than they had ever been before. The roses were especially beautiful; they were so brilliant they seemed to almost glow. Everyone came up to admire them.

"Isn't this amazing?" I exclaimed. "When I was here, the garden didn't bloom like this. These flowers are so beautiful."

"You know why?" my mother said. "It's because Amah watered them with her tears."

"So you see," Mom said. "Even the oldest person cries when she misses someone."

I nodded and looked out the window, as a tear rolled down my nose.

Chapter 13

School Without Melody

our class quilt

AFTER MELODY LEFT, I THOUGHT EVERYTHING would be over and life wouldn't go on. But it did. I still took the school bus to school, Ms. Magon kept giving homework and spelling tests, Lissy kept complaining about her hair, Ki-Ki kept asking for Barbie dolls, Dad still went to work, and Mom still made dinner. But it was odd.

In school, Mr. Valente finally sewed our poem quilt and we hung it at the back of the room. He put Melody's and my squares right next to each other. When I saw it, I felt happy and sad about that at the same time. Happy because I knew that we'd be remembered in school together forever, but sad because it reminded me that Melody was gone.

But I missed Melody the most when Ms. Magon told us about the last project of the year.

"Our last project is going to be a free project," Ms. Magon said. "I want to finish our study of the Vikings by having you all choose your project."

"What do you mean—choose your project?" Becky asked.

"I mean you can do whatever you want, as long as it is about the Vikings. You can build a model Viking ship, you can dress up like a Viking and tell us about them, anything you want," Ms. Magon said. "You can have a partner or work by yourself, whichever you prefer. But remember, if you have a partner, I want to see double the work."

Melody's empty desk

When Ms. Magon said that, I felt myself drooping in my seat. Usually, I loved when we got partner projects because that meant Melody and I could work together. But now, as I looked at Melody's empty desk, I felt lost.

"Hey, do you want to work with me and Charlotte?" Becky asked me. "We're going to build a Viking ship out of candy. Ms. Magon would probably let us be three partners."

I shook my head. I didn't want to make a Viking ship out of candy and I didn't want to be a third partner either.

"I don't know," I said. "I'm still thinking about what I'm going to do."

"Aren't you going to make a book?" Charlotte asked. "You always make a book."

That was true. Ever since I had found my talent and decided that I wanted to be an author and illustrator, I made a book for every school project. No matter what the topic, I made a book. For the science fair, I made a book about clouds. For geography class, I made a book about West Virginia. Even the salesperson at the local copy store where Mom got my book bound knew us. He always smiled when we walked through the door and said to me, "Another masterpiece?"

Books I authored and illustrated

"I'm not sure," I told Charlotte. "Maybe."

"Really?" Becky said. "Well, if you don't make a book, you should make a candy boat with us."

I watched the two of them in their seats, planning their boat. I felt confused. Maybe I should be a third partner with Charlotte and Becky and make a candy boat. But it just didn't feel right. But then, nothing felt right—not even making a book. Maybe wanting to be an author and illustrator was another thing that was going to change.

Dun-Wei

Dun-Wei

"DID YOU KNOW," BECKY TOLD ME THAT DAY AT recess, "there's a new boy in Mrs. Sherman's class. He's Chinese, like you."

Suddenly, I remembered. The Chinese family that took Melody's house! The enemy! They were here! I tried to stay calm.

"Oh, really?" I said.

"Well," Becky cocked her head, "he's not exactly like you. He's from China and he doesn't speak any English. Everyone thinks he's weird."

"Weird how?" I asked.

"Audrey said that when Mrs. Sherman came into the room, he stood up like he was in the army. And he's always bowing his head, like there's something wrong with his neck," Becky said. "His name is Dun-Wei Liu. Look, they're already making fun of him."

I followed Becky's pointing hand across the playground. Yes, there was an Asian boy. Kurt and Rich were with him. Kurt and Rich were always trying to be funny and would pick on people. They would yell "Fire" at Jenny Hansen's red hair and say it burned them or call Joe Elly "Smelly Elly" and pretend he smelled bad. When we were in kindergarten they used to stretch their eyes with their fingers and chant pretend Chinese at me. I never said anything, and after a while it got boring for them so they stopped. No one remembered that now. Except for me.

Kurt and Rich make fun of Joe Elly

Dun-Wei's
lunch box

Dun-Wei was an easy target. It wasn't just because he was new. He did look weird, though I wasn't sure why. He didn't have strange hair or crazy clothes, but there were all these small things that weren't right. His pants were a little too short and his socks just seemed too white. His jacket matched brand-new sneakers and he carried a lunch box instead of a brown paper bag like everyone else did. These were just little things, but somehow, all those little wrong things made him stick out like a big mistake. Even though I had been ready to hate him because he had taken Melody's house, when I saw him I didn't feel that way.

"Dumb-WAAAY!" Rich called out. "Which way is the dumbest way?"

Kurt joined in and a lot of the boys started laughing. Dun-Wei took a look at them and his face turned red. He wasn't dumb at all. He knew they were making fun of him. He shouted something back which no one understood and just made them tease and laugh harder.

Even though we were far away, I could tell something bad was going to happen. As the laughter grew louder, the scowl on Dun-Wei's face grew blacker. He tightened his grip on his lunch box and started swinging. BANG! He hit Rich! BANG! He hit Kurt! The boys stopped laughing and they jumped on him.

"FIGHT! FIGHT!" everyone started yelling.

Luckily, a whistle cut through the air and a recess teacher ran over and stopped everything. We watched her march all three of them into the school. When they passed us, I saw Dun-Wei look at me with surprise and hope, but I turned away as fast as possible. I felt all mixed up—confused and ashamed and guilty and scared. Even if he was the enemy, I knew the

in trouble after the fight

66

whole thing wasn't right. But I didn't want people to think I was like him—odd and strange and all wrong. I didn't want everyone to think that we were the same because we were both Asian.

"Wow, that was a fight," Charlotte said. "Kurt and Rich are going to get in trouble."

"Yeah," Becky said. "Those boys are so bad. Doesn't Rich have the cutest smile, though?"

I looked at Becky and Charlotte in surprise. They seemed excited and almost happy about the fight. Even though they chattered on about how bad Rich and Kurt were, I could tell they were thrilled by them. They didn't think about Dun-Wei at all; it was almost as if he didn't even matter. The fear I felt before seemed to turn into an icy wind howling in my stomach, and suddenly I knew there was one thing I was not confused about. I didn't want to be like Dun-Wei, without friends and easily forgotten.

"Hey," I said to Becky, interrupting their conversation. "I changed my mind. I'll be a third partner. I want to make that candy boat with you guys, after all."

Chapter 15

Fresh off the Boat

my rice bowl

DUN-WEI, RICH, AND KURT WERE PUNISHED FOR fighting by getting an "in-school suspension." That meant they still had to come to school, but had to do all their work in a separate room away from their classes. They weren't allowed to see anyone and no one saw them. But everyone talked about them.

Becky and Charlotte talked about Kurt and Rich the most. I knew they would like it if Rich and Kurt liked them. And I kind of understood why. Rich *was* cute. And if he liked you and was nice to you, that would mean you were special because you would be the only one he'd be nice to. Somehow, him being mean to everyone else except for you would make you special. But even though that made sense, it still seemed backward to me; sometimes I felt like my head hurt from trying to figure it out. The whole thing made me feel strange. I just wanted to forget about it, but the next day at dinner I knew that wouldn't be possible.

"Pacy," Mom said. "Why didn't you tell me there was a new Chinese boy in school?"

I shrugged.

"The school called me up today and asked me to talk to him and his family," Mom said, "since they just came from China, and Dad and I speak Chinese. His family invited us to come over for dinner. Pacy, I want you to be friends with him."

I looked up, alarmed. "Do I have to?"

"Why not?" Mom said.

"I don't know," I mumbled, looking down at my plate. "He's kind of weird."

"Weird, how?" Mom pushed.

I didn't know what to say. I looked at the grains of rice sticking to the end of my chopsticks in mushy clumps. If I squinted my eyes, I could pretend they were mashed potatoes.

"Aww," Lissy said, breaking in. "Don't make Pacy be friends with him. It's hard enough fitting in without being friends with someone fresh off the boat."

"What's that mean, fresh off the boat?" Ki-Ki asked.

"You know, fresh off the boat," Lissy said. "That's what they call people who just came here from another country and don't know how to be American yet."

"It doesn't sound like you call them that in a nice way," Mom said. "It seems like people say that in a mean way."

"I guess so," Lissy said, considering, "because they are the ones everyone thinks are nerds and looks down on."

"Well, that's wrong!" Mom said sharply. We all looked up, surprised. Mom rarely spoke like that. She looked at us seriously. "It's very hard to come to a new country, and it's even harder when others judge you harshly. You feel ashamed, in a way that you can never forget. I know I'll never forget my mistake with the canned meat."

CANNED MEAT

Even though Dad and I had studied English for six years in Taiwan, when we came to the United States it was as if we knew nothing. Every day in my college class, I was so confused. I could never understand what the professor was saying; his words seemed to fly by me like sparrows, and if I could catch one or two, it was like grabbing feathers in the wind.

Mom in her
college class

I was desperate to do better. So I decided that I would pack myself two meals and spend the whole day in the library studying. But even the simplest things, like making myself food, were hard.

Buying food in Taiwan was different than in the United States. Our supermarket in Taiwan was a building with hundreds of vendors with their own stands inside, each one calling out for people to buy their goods. It was always full of people crowded together, like the pearls in

Mom in the grocery store

tapioca pudding. There was always someone smiling and talking, trying to show you the best fruit or the best deal. In America, the grocery store was big and cold and empty, with aisles full of food that seemed to go on like a maze.

And I didn't know what to buy. Everything was pack-aged differently and I had a hard time reading the words. I needed to buy something that would be easy to bring with me and also inexpen-sive, because Dad and I didn't have that much money.

I finally stopped in an aisle where there were all kinds of canned meat and fish. It was so cheap! In Taiwan, canned fish was a treat—an expensive delicacy. I was eager to try this American kind. But there were so many brands. I wasn't sure which one to get. Finally, I chose the brand with a tiger on it. In Taiwan, there was a "Lucky Tiger" brand of meat; I thought maybe this was the American version.

So the next day, I got up very early and went to the

library to study. There were some students in my class sitting at the table across from me, but they didn't talk to me, so I sat alone. At lunchtime, I took out my canned meat, opened it, and tried some with my chopsticks. Yuck! No wonder it was so cheap; it tasted horrible.

But then I heard a loud noise of disgust. I looked up and saw one of the girls from my class looking at me like I was a dirty cockroach. She closed her book loudly, pulled at her friend's sleeve, and turned around to leave, as if she couldn't bear the sight of me. While I couldn't understand the English of my professor's lectures or salesclerks at the store, her words were clear in my ears.

canned meat

"That's so gross," she said to her friend. "Those Chinese will eat anything."

I dropped my chopsticks, gathered my books and food, and rushed home, tears burning in my eyes like boiling oil. When Dad got home, I told him the story and we looked at the canned meat together. And slowly, we figured out why my classmate was disgusted. That canned meat was cat food!

"I was so embarrassed and horrified," Mom finished. "I'll never forget how ashamed I felt."

"You really ate cat food?" I said. It would've been funny if Mom hadn't felt so bad about it.

"Yes," Mom said. "Things got better after that, but it took a long time. That's why you should be more understanding of people who are 'fresh off the boat.' It's easy to make mistakes and it's hard to fit in."

Mom's story made me feel sad. And I hoped when we went over to Dun-Wei's house they wouldn't serve us cat food for dinner.

Chapter 16

Dinner with the Enemy

incense

THAT WEEKEND WE WENT OVER TO DUN-WEI'S house for dinner. I dreaded it. I tried to make excuses for why I couldn't go, but Mom wouldn't listen to me. Even when I said I had too much homework and needed to study, that didn't work, and that almost always worked. Instead, all she did was fuss at us about our manners.

"When we are having dinner, don't play with your chopsticks," Mom said to us as she covered a box of chocolates in ladybug-red paper. They were the good kind of chocolates, the ones with lots of nuts and crunchy toffee, and they came wrapped in gold foil. We were going to give them to Dun-Wei's family.

Lucky them! "And don't pretend your chopsticks are drumsticks, like you do at home. That is bad manners."

"Okay, okay," we said, bored by her instructions.

"And only put them on your plate; don't put your chopsticks on the table," Mom said. "And don't stick your chopsticks straight up in your rice bowl either."

"Yes," Dad said. "That's very bad. It reminds people of incense sticks at temples."

"Isn't incense good?" Lissy asked.

"Good for when you are honoring spirits," Dad said. "Not for when you are honoring your stomach."

When we got to the house, I felt weird. It was strange going to Melody's house with someone else living there. Everything was the same, but different. It was the same brown house, but Melody's stained-glass unicorn wasn't in the window and her brother's toy trucks weren't on the lawn. Even though a cheerful yellow light glowed from the windows, I felt like the house was abandoned.

Melody's stained-glass unicorn

But the door burst open as soon as we rang the

doorbell, and Dun-Wei and his parents welcomed us in.

"Ni hao, ni hao ma," they said, bowing as we came in. That means "Hello! How are you?"

Dun–Wei bowed to me. He didn't smile, but he didn't act unfriendly either. Still, I didn't trust it. I gave him a small bow back. You never knew what to expect with the enemy.

"Ja-ba, bei?" Lissy said, trying to show off.

Dun-Wei and his parents looked puzzled until Dad said something in Chinese. Then they all laughed.

"What's so funny?" Lissy asked.

"You just got things confused," Mom said. "Ja-ba, bei is Taiwanese, not Chinese. The Lius didn't know what you were saying."

Mrs. Liu pushed us toward the dining room, through the kitchen. Everything was different from when Melody lived there. All of Melody's stickers had been scraped off the cabinets and the dog magnets we used to play with on the refrigerator were gone. And right near the stove, above the dull metal wok and knife with a blade shaped like a brick, a red picture hung. It was a printed picture of a Chinese man from ancient times. Underneath what I thought was a helmet with wings, he had a large white and pinkish-purple face. Later, Mom told me that it was a picture of the Kitchen God, a Chinese God that watched over the family. I could believe that; I felt like his black eyes were watching me the whole time. I hur-

picture of Kitchen God at Dun-Wei's house

ried into the dining room to get away from them.

The dining table was covered with food. There was fried shrimp with salt like crystals, dandelion-yellow stained chicken stuffed with rice, light brown

Corn on the cob

pork buns, stir-fried vegetables and noodles, a fish with mushrooms and meat, a moon-colored soup, cotton-white steamed rice and corn on the cob.

"Corn on the cob!" I said, surprised. I couldn't help giggling a little. It seemed so out of place on the table full of Chinese food. "That's funny."

"I like corn on the cob," Lissy said quicky. I could tell

she was afraid I was being rude. "We eat it all the time in the summer."

"Yes," Mr. Liu said and nodded at her. "In China, too."

"Really?" I said. "I thought corn on the cob was American."

"But we eat it in China too," Mr. Liu told me. "People sell it on the street—like hot dogs."

"Yes," Mom said. "They do that in Taiwan, too."

"Really?" I said. It seemed so strange to think that Chinese and Taiwanese people ate food that I thought was completely American. But I was still glad to eat it.

And that was what I did all through dinner. The parents laughed and talked in Chinese, so all Lissy, Ki-Ki, and I did was eat, since we didn't understand any of it. Dun-Wei didn't say much. Once or twice, Lissy tried to say something to him, but he just shook his head. He couldn't understand us either.

"Dun-Wei," Mr. Liu said to him once. "Try to speak English."

Dun-Wei just looked down at his plate. And Mr. Liu said something to Mom and Dad in Chinese. They made sympathetic noises, and I knew they were talking about Dun-Wei. He knew so, too, because his scowl was like the black ink of a squid, dark and hostile. For a moment I was scared; it looked like the enemy was going to attack.

Dun-Wei scowling

But Mr. Liu said, "Why don't you kids go to the other room? We rented some movies you can watch."

The blackness on Dun-Wei's face cleared away as we left the table. We went into the TV room, which used to be Melody's Dad's office. Dun-Wei took out the movies and held them out to me. I chose the one about a superhero. We had seen it already, but I didn't mind seeing it again. I wondered how Dun-Wei would like it, considering he couldn't understand what they were saying.

But he seemed to enjoy it, because he laughed at all the funny parts with us. Maybe he knew more

English then he let on. Anyway, by the time the super-hero had destroyed the evil monster robot, it was time to go home. Dun-Wei got our coats and the Liu family bowed as we thanked them and said good-bye.

As we got into the car, I yawned; I was full and tired and ready for bed. Dinner with Dun-Wei and his family hadn't been that bad after all. In fact, for the enemy, they seemed a lot like us.

my birthday
cake

SPRING AND SUMMER WERE NOW BLENDING together. The ground was no longer a mix of seaweed-colored grass and mud that felt like wet tea leaves at the bottom of a cup. The gray rain stopped and white clouds dotted the sky. It was May, and that meant my birthday was coming!

Mom said that in Taiwan, they didn't have birthday parties for kids, only for adults, so I knew I had to pay attention to make sure we did everything right. For my birthday this year, we were going to go see a play. The high school drama club was putting on a play called *Anne of the Thousand Days*, which was about the Queen of England a long time ago. All the girls in my class were going to come over to my house for

my birthday party invitations

cake and presents and then Mom was going to drive us to the high school to see the play. I felt like this was the right way to have my party, since I was getting too old to have a party where we played games.

Even though I knew I could make my own invitations better than the ones they had in the store, I bought the ones with balloons on them and sent those. Mom tried to help by buying a cookbook that had recipes for cakes and cookies, but I thought it was too risky to have her make something. She never baked American things like that, just Chinese food like steamed buns and taro tapioca. In fact, the only time Mom used her cake tin was when she made *lo bak go*, a salty radish cake that you fried

Mom's radish cake

83

and ate with soy sauce. And I couldn't have THAT at my party. So, instead, we ordered a cake from Hemstrought's Bakery. It had blue flowers and "Happy Birthday Grace" written in matching icing on the top. I wanted everything to be perfect.

And it looked like I was going to get my wish. Mom got soda, caramel corn, and potato chips, and every girl that was invited came—except, of course, Melody.

"You know how *Anne of the Thousand Days* is supposed to be a love story about the King and Queen of England?" Becky asked. "Heather Smele, the girl that plays Anne, and David Williams, the boy who plays the king, are boyfriend and girlfriend in real life."

"Oooh, that's so cute," Charlotte said. "They are perfect together. They're both blond and tall. No wonder they got those parts. They're the cutest couple in the high school."

"Who do you think would be the cutest couple in our grade?" one of the girls asked.

David Williams and Heather Smele in the play ANNE OF THE THOUSAND DAYS

"Well, you and Jerry Lucelli would be cute," Charlotte said. "You both have curly brown hair."

"You and Rich would be really cute," Becky told Charlotte. "You both have the cutest smiles."

All the girls started giggling and we began pairing everyone up in our grade. It was fun until I heard Charlotte say she thought Alice would be a cute couple with Sam Mercer. I liked Sam! I wanted him to be a cute couple with me.

"Who do you think I'd be a cute couple with?" I asked.

"Hmm, I don't know," Charlotte said. "Maybe Dun-Wei?"

"Dumb-Way! Charlotte, don't say that," Becky said. "That's not nice. Who'd want to be a cute couple with Dumb-Way?"

"Noo, I was only saying that because you're both Chinese," Charlotte protested. "It's hard to match you in a cute couple. You don't fit anyone else."

Suddenly, I felt like a flower wilting. Was it true? Was the only boy I'd ever be a cute couple with Dun-Wei? Would nobody else ever like me because I was Chinese? And I wasn't even really Chinese either! It wasn't fair! I felt angry—angry at Charlotte for saying it, angry at Dun-Wei for being fresh off the boat, and angry at myself because I was Taiwanese. Suddenly, I didn't want a party anymore; I just wanted everyone to go away.

"Happy birthday!" Mom sang as she came through the door with my cake. It was all lit up and everyone joined the song. Even though everyone was smiling and laughing, I felt like crying. When it was time for me to make my wish, a hundred wishes filled my head and mixed into one. I wished for the party to be over, for Dun-Wei not to have come to my school, for Melody not to have moved, and for me not to be Chinese or Taiwanese. But most of all, I wished the Year of the Rat, with all its changes, had never come.

Chapter 18

Library Book

using my library option

AFTER MY BIRTHDAY, I STARTED USING MY LIBRARY option again. Library option was when you chose to read in the library instead of going out to the playground. I had used it all the time with Melody, but since she left I had gone out on the playground to be with Charlotte and Becky. Now I felt like not going to the playground was a good way to avoid Dun-Wei, as well as the uncomfortable feeling I had with Becky and Charlotte.

Whenever I was with them I always felt like a shoe on the wrong foot, somehow not fitting. It was strange because I had never felt like that with them before Melody had come and gone. Before, nothing they talked about ever bothered me, and we all used to laugh together. But now, sometimes, especially when they talked about Kurt and Rich, they annoyed me—like mosquito bites on my back that I couldn't reach. I wasn't sure what had changed.

So using my library option was a relief. Besides, I loved reading. Our class had a reading contest called "Shoot for the Moon!" There was a big bulletin board with everyone's name on it on one side and a cutout

The Shoot for the Moon contest Bulletin Board

of the moon on the other side. For every book you finished, Ms. Magon put a star with the book's title and your book summary next to your name. The goal was to get so many stars lined up next to your name that it reached the moon. Everyone who reached the moon got a prize.

Before, Melody and I had wanted to reach the moon together and would wait for each other before we put a star up. But since she wasn't here anymore, I just read as fast as I could, so my line of stars grew and grew. It made me a little sad to see my line stretch out way past Melody's. I guessed Melody would never reach the moon.

The book I was reading now was *Harriet the Spy*. It

HARRIET THE SPY book

was a good book; Harriet wanted to be an author like me. She wrote everything down in a notebook. I thought that was a good idea; maybe I'd get Mom to buy me a notebook so I could do the

same. When the bell rang at the end of recess, I didn't want to put the book away. How was it going to end? I decided to borrow it and take it home to finish.

I couldn't wait to finish it. I read it in the car when we took Ki-Ki to her violin recital, in the dressing room when Lissy was trying on her new jeans, and finally finished it on the way to the post office when I mailed the Cheerleaders book back to Melody. I really liked it, even though I thought Harriet was careless to lose her notebook. I wouldn't have lost mine.

But on Monday morning before school, I couldn't find the book. Where had I put it? I checked everywhere: under the bed, on the sofa, in the kitchen. It wasn't in any of those places. Where was it?

The day passed, then a week, and then another, and I still couldn't find it. And then one day, Ms. Magon handed me a pink slip of paper. It was an overdue notice! It said *Harriet the Spy* had to be returned IMMEDIATELY. What was I going to do? I was so

LIBRARY OVERDUE NOTICE

Grace Lin   Room 301

YOUR LIBRARY BOOK IS OVERDUE

Name of Book *Harriet The Spy*

Author *Louise Fitzhugh*

Date *May 28th*

* return IMMEDIATELY

worried; I stopped using my library option because I was afraid our librarian, Ms. McCurdy, would ask me about the book.

When I showed Mom my overdue notice she shook her head.

"I told you I won't clean your room anymore," she said. "You are old enough to take care of that yourself. I'm sure it's in there somewhere. It's a mess."

I didn't think my room was a mess. I thought it was cozy, just like a mouse nest or squirrel's hole before winter. But maybe Mom was right and it was in there somewhere. I spent the whole night cleaning and organizing it. By the time I was done I had found a box of pink, green, and blue colored erasers that smelled like candy, my glitter unicorn stickers, my silver star bicycle bell, and my socks with the dogs on them. But no book!

After I got my second overdue notice, Mom said she would look for me. So all day when I was at school, Mom cleaned and searched the house. No luck!

"You probably dropped it somewhere," Mom said. "The only thing you can do is tell the library you lost it."

I didn't want to do that! What if Ms. McCurdy yelled at me? Would Ms. Magon take down all my stars, saying that I didn't deserve to reach the moon because I lost the book? I probably wouldn't ever be allowed to take a book out of the library again.

But I had to. The next morning I received my third overdue notice. And it said, "Please see Ms. McCurdy immediately" in red ink at the bottom. I gulped.

At the library, Ms. McCurdy looked at me from behind her glasses.

"Grace," she said crisply, "*Harriet the Spy* is over a month overdue. Holly Honchell in Mrs. Robinson's class has been waiting for it."

"Um," I stammered. "I think I lost the book."

"Oh dear," Ms. McCurdy said. "Are you sure?"

I nodded.

"Well," she said, "I'm afraid you'll have to pay the library to get a new one."

"How much will it cost?" I asked.

"Hmm." Ms. McCurdy started to type some letters on the computer. "Ten dollars and eighty-five cents." $10.85! That was a lot of money. Two years ago I won fourth place in a book contest and won $400. I guessed I would have to take the money from that.

When I got home, Mom counted my money for me.

I only had $11.40 left from my prize.

"I used to be rich!" I said. "What happened?"

"You spent it," Mom said, "remember? You bought a new bike, you and Melody went to the state fair, the bookstore, the art store. It all adds up."

I guess it did. The next day I paid for my book, and during library option, instead of reading I figured out how much money I had left. I only had $.55. That wasn't a lot of money at all. I wasn't rich anymore. Now I was poor. A sad feeling came over me, like gray rain on my birthday. I was so unlucky!

When I got home, there was a package waiting for me. It was from Melody. That made me feel better. I opened it up and there was—

MY LOST LIBRARY BOOK!

I couldn't believe it. That's where the book was this whole time! I must have mailed it to her by mistake when I sent her the Cheerleaders books. And she had read it, too. I wondered if Ms. Magon would add a new star next to Melody's name.

Dear Pacy,

I got the Cheerleaders books, thanks!
after I'm done reading them again, I'll
send them back. I also read Harriet the
Spy. You sent it to me with the
Cheerleaders book. It was a good book.
I thought it was too bad that she lost her
notebook and all her friends got mad
at her though. Anyway, when I got to
the end I saw the library sticker and
I think you sent me the book by
mistake. So I'm sending it back before
I send the Cheerleaders books. I
hope you don't get in trouble for sending
me the book. It is hot here in California.
We are having a water shortage, which
means we can't take long showers. I
will tell you about it later. How is
Sam Mercer?

Your friend,

Melody

Chapter 19

Bad Grade

Viking ship made
out of candy

EVEN THOUGH I HAD FOUND MY LIBRARY BOOK,
I still felt like my tiger luck had left me, because
when Ms. Magon handed Charlotte, Becky, and me
our grades on the Viking project, we got a C+! That
was the lowest grade I had ever gotten. What would
Mom and Dad say? Ms. Magon wrote on our paper,
"The candy boat was very cute, but it didn't show me
what you knew about the Vikings. Also, it didn't look
like there was enough work done for a three-person
project."

"Are your parents going to get mad at you for not
getting an A?" Charlotte asked when she saw my face.
"You always get A's. They shouldn't get mad because
you got a bad grade once."

That was true. And the more I thought about it, the more I began to think Charlotte was right. Mom and Dad were too picky. One bad grade was not a big deal.

Unfortunately, Mom didn't think that way at all. When I told her about my grade (Dad wasn't home yet), she looked at me very seriously. I knew I was in trouble.

"You got a C!" Mom said. "That's not very good. What happened?"

"I don't know," I said defensively. "Ms. Magon just gave me one."

"There must be a reason," Mom said. "You should have done much better."

"I don't know why you think it's such a big deal!" I burst out. "Everyone gets bad grades in my class. I don't always have to get A's!"

"It's not about the grade," Mom said. "Tell the truth, did you do the best you could on the project?

I wanted to say yes, but I thought about all the times I went over to Becky's house. We were supposed to be working on the project, but most

making the candy boat

of the time they just talked about Kurt and Rich while I ate candy. We didn't really work that hard on the project at all.

"I don't care about the grade," Mom said, "IF you worked your hardest and put all your effort into it."

"You do too care about the grade," I argued. "What if I didn't work at all and got an A? You wouldn't say anything then."

"Pacy," Mom said. "You are not looking at this the right way. I want you to get good grades and do well in school, not for me, but for you. I want you to grow up and be able to do whatever you want. Getting good grades and learning things is the key to any door you want to open in the future. If you don't try your best, you are hurting yourself the most."

This made me think. Mom talking about doors reminded me about how being an author and illustrator was a "cold door." Was getting good grades the key to opening it? Even though I wasn't sure if I wanted to go through the cold door, I still wanted to be able to open it. I could always change my mind after the door was open. But if it was locked, I wouldn't even get the choice. Still, I didn't want to admit Mom was right.

"Well, trying my best all the time is hard," I said. "And if it's for me, then I don't mind if I get a bad grade once in a while."

"Well, then I mind for you," Mom said. "Which is why I care about your grades. Maybe I care more about you than you care about yourself."

And, strangely, even though Mom said that in an angry voice, that made me feel kind of happy inside. I liked knowing that Mom was looking out for me. Suddenly, I realized, even if I was unlucky and my tiger luck left me, Mom never would. And that wouldn't ever change.

"Am I going be punished?" I asked.

Mom gave me a funny smile and sighed. She sat down next to me. "Did I ever tell you about when I was punished for my bad grades?" Mom asked.

THE PUNISHMENT

When I was your age, I was punished for my grades all the time. Not by my parents, but by my teachers. Remember when I told you that schools in Taiwan were different from schools here? Well, they were very different, in some ways that were not nice.

One of my teachers was especially strict and ruthless. Everything about her was mean. She was ugly, like a witch, and when she smiled it was like a dog baring its teeth to attack. Every morning, after test days, the teacher would call us up, one by one, and beat our hands with a stick. The number of questions we got wrong on the test was the number of times she'd beat us.

One of my friends, Yan, lived in special fear of our teacher. Yan tried very hard, but whenever our tests came, she could not pass. Every day I studied with her, for hours, trying to help her. "I wish I were smart like you," she would say to me, wistfully. "I would do anything to be smarter." And she did try everything. She would sleep with her books and rewrite math problems over and over again, but it didn't seem to help.

One day, the teacher surprised us by handing our test papers back to us without a beating. Yan and I looked at each other, hopeful that perhaps we would escape punishment. But we should have known better.

"Everyone who didn't have a perfect score, stand up!" she barked after everyone received their papers. "I want you to slap your face and keep slapping."

students hitting themselves

We did as we were told. "Harder, Yi," she ordered out to a student who wasn't hitting herself with enough strength. "Faster, Jia Li!" she yelled at another. Only when our faces were as pink as lychee skins did she nod, grim and satisfied.

"Okay," she said, "those with only one wrong answer on their tests can stop and sit down." And then she would wait another two excruciating minutes and then let those with only two wrong answers sit down. And then, after that, those with three answers wrong could sit down, and so on. When I was lucky enough to sit down, I watched in horror as Yan stood for what seemed like hours, beating herself. Her face throbbed blood red from soreness and embarrassment as she was singled out as the stupidest in the class. Yan's eyes shone with tears, like a helpless dog about to be run over by a train.

But when she looked at me, it wasn't a look for help. It was a look of yearning. I knew she was wishing that she could be like me, smart enough to remember the answers after studying, smart enough to answer questions correctly, smart enough to sit down. Even today, I can remember poor Yan's red face with her pathetic eyes burning.

When I was promoted to the next grade with a different teacher, sometimes I would be tempted to not study as hard. But I would remember Yan and how hard she studied and how much she envied me, and I would feel ashamed.

"That is why it's very important that you always try your best," Mom said. "Yan tried so hard, yet couldn't pass the test. She would've done anything to be able to get a good grade. For you not to get a good grade because you are lazy is shameful. And that, if anything, is what deserves punishment."

"That's horrible," I said. "The police should've arrested that teacher!"

"Things were different back then," Mom said. "They're better now, but the idea that you should work hard is still the same."

I guessed since things were different, not all changes were that bad. I was glad Ms. Magon wasn't anything like Mom's old teacher.

"So, will you promise to work harder?" Mom said. "And no more bad grades because of laziness?"

I agreed.

church

THE LEAVES AND LAWN SPARKLED GREEN LIKE emerald jewels, and our yellow school bus that dropped us off for the last time that year looked like a sunflower on the street. School was finally over, summer was here, and that meant we were going to Clifford's wedding! He was going to get married in Boston, Massachusetts, where his other grandparents lived (our grandparents lived in Taiwan; it was the other side of the family). I had never been to Boston before. Everyone said it was a good place to eat beans; I didn't know why. But even though I didn't like beans, I couldn't wait to go.

Ki-Ki was going to be a flower girl. I was jealous.

Ki-Ki in her
flower girl dress

Mom bought her a special white dress with lace that fluffed out, and she was going to carry a basket of flowers. It was almost as good as being the bride.

The night before the wedding, we stayed at a hotel near Clifford's grandparents' house. It was fun staying at a hotel. The only bad thing about staying there was that I had to share a bed with Lissy. She kicked!

our hotel room

In the morning, Mom rushed us to get ready for the wedding. We had to be there early since Ki-Ki was a flower girl. Ki-Ki got to wear her new flower-girl dress while Lissy and I had to wear our silk Chinese dresses with the tight collars. Lissy had grown so much that Mom bought her a new dress, too. It was deep sapphire blue and embroidered with silver-gold bamboo leaves.

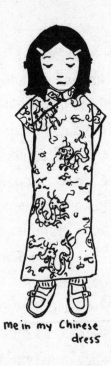

me in my Chinese dress

I didn't like my dress. It was bright green, the color of steamed broccoli, with gold dragons all over it. It was Lissy's old dress that she grew out of. She had picked it for the dragons especially, but I thought dragons should be on boys' clothes, not a girl's dress. And I didn't think it was fair that I was the only one that had to wear an old dress to the wedding.

"My dress is old, too," Mom said, when I complained. Her dress was green-blue silk.

"That's not the same," I said. "Yours doesn't count."

"Why not?" Mom asked, laughing.

"Because," I said, "you're Mom!"

Lissy, Mom, Dad, and I went to go sit in the pews while Aunt Linda, Clifford's mother, pinned flowers onto Mom and Dad and rushed Ki-Ki to the back for photographs. The church was full of people. Everyone was talking and laughing so fast that it sounded like hundreds of clicking chopsticks. I could barely hear the organ music playing.

Suddenly, without warning, everyone quieted down. Clifford (who looked really funny in his tuxedo), his groomsmen, and the priest had walked out and were standing at the altar. The lively organ music changed to slow booming chords. The wedding was going to begin!

First Clifford's parents came down the aisle and then Lian's mother. Then, Ki-Ki and the other flower girl, Ting Ting, walked down the aisle. Ki-Ki's mouth made a straight line and she was clutching her basket so tightly that her knuckles were turning the same color as her dress. But she and Ting Ting made it to the altar without any problem. Of course, if there had been any problems, Older Cousin Hannah and the other bridesmaids (in their gleaming gold dresses) would have done something, because they were walking right behind them.

And then the music changed to a stately march and everyone stood up. Here came the bride! Lian was so pretty. Her black hair was braided and curled on her head, and her dark eyes sparkled like the diamond ring on her hand. Her long veil covered her, and her dress was a waterfall of lace trailing behind her. I didn't know why she was marrying goofy Clifford; she seemed much too pretty for him.

When she got to the altar, Lian and Clifford faced each other with the priest in between them. They smiled at each other like they had just eaten a warm egg custard on a cold day. And suddenly I realized that once Clifford was married, he wouldn't be just our favorite cousin anymore; he'd be grown-up—he'd be Lian's husband, with a house and car like Uncle Leo. I sat straight up. Clifford was going to change right in front of me.

But then the priest started speaking in Taiwanese! He was marrying them in Taiwanese and I couldn't understand a thing he was saying. I slumped down. This wasn't that much fun. I had to wear an old dress, I didn't get any flowers, no one wanted to take my photo, and now I couldn't understand the ceremony. Clifford was changing and I wasn't a part of it.

Mom nudged me to sit up. I straightened up again and tried not to be rude. The dark wood of the pew was smooth and warm against my fingers; the light from the stained glass windows cast a glow on the guests and our Chinese silk dresses shimmered. I watched a tear run down Aunt Linda's cheek, leaving a trail of black from her make-up. She was smiling, though, so I knew they were what people called "tears of joy." I always thought that was strange. I never cried when I was happy. But I guessed this meant Aunt Linda was happy about Clifford changing, so maybe this

Aunt Linda

change wasn't that bad either. The minister droned on and on.

Finally, Lian was talking and then Clifford. This was it; it was almost official . . . and then it was! Clifford kissed Lian and everyone stood up and clapped and cheered. Clifford was married!

Chapter 21

Clifford's Chinese Reception

Butterfly Hair pin

AFTER THE CHURCH CEREMONY, WE DROVE TO A Chinese restaurant called China Pearl. Clifford had rented the whole restaurant for the evening! I guess he needed to because there were so many guests.

Lissy, Ki-Ki, and I followed Mom to the private room where Lian was changing. All the women were there helping. They clucked around Lian like chickens waiting to be fed.

"Hello!" Lian said to us, as we came in. "I guess I'm your new cousin!" Lian spoke English like Mom. You could understand what she was saying, but she had an accent.

She was changing into a shining red Chinese dress.

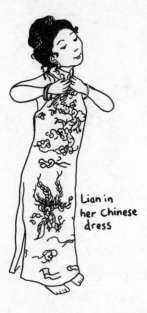

Lian in her Chinese dress

I knew red was a Chinese lucky color, so I wasn't surprised it was the color of a brilliant ruby. A gold and silver dragon and a bird were embroidered on it.

"The bird is a phoenix," Lian said, when she saw me staring at her dress. "It's traditional for Chinese weddings because a dragon symbolizes the groom and a phoenix symbolizes the bride."

That made me wish even more that my dress didn't have dragons on it; I knew dragons were for boys.

From a leaf-green silk-covered box, Aunt Linda took out a fancy Chinese hairpin in the shape of a butterfly. The wings looked as if they were made of gold thread and the green jade stones on it looked like shiny jelly beans. I almost wanted to taste them.

"Who should fix Lian's hair?" Aunt Linda asked.

"I'll do it!" I said. I thought it'd be fun and then I could be a part of the wedding, too. But everyone laughed.

"No," Cousin Hannah told me. "It has to be a lucky adult woman. Someone who has parents, a husband, and kids that are alive, healthy, and happy."

"It's so the woman's good luck will be passed on to the bride," Aunt Linda said. "I think your mom should do it."

Mom protested, because she was nervous about fixing Lian's hair. "I don't want to make it ugly!" she said. But everyone insisted.

But just as Mom was putting the fragile butterfly in Lian's hair, there was a loud knock at the door.

"Hello?" Clifford called.

"We'd better take care of this," Cousin Hannah said to Lian's mother with a wink. As they left, Lian and Aunt Linda laughed as if there was a joke. Lissy and I looked at each other, puzzled, so we went too—followed by Ki-Ki, Ting Ting, and some other bridesmaids.

"You know you have to pay up if you want to see your bride," Cousin Hannah said to Clifford. "What do you have for us?"

"You're not really going to make me pay, are you?" Clifford asked. "That old tradition? C'mon, let me in!"

"Nope," Cousin Hannah said. "We're waiting."

At first, I was surprised that Cousin Hannah was being so mean, but her eyes were twinkling and I could see that everyone was trying hard not to smile and laugh. This must've been the joke.

"Okay," Clifford said. "Here's nine dollars and ninety-nine cents."

"Nine dollars and ninety-nine cents!" Cousin Hannah said. "Are you crazy? Is that what your bride is worth to you?!"

"Hey, it's 999," Clifford said, "I've tripled the lucky number nine!"

"Why is nine a lucky number?" Lissy asked.

Clifford pays

"Because it sounds like the Chinese word for 'forever,'" Clifford told us. "So nine dollars and ninety-nine cents means forever times three!"

"Cheapskate," Hannah said. "I'm ashamed we're related."

"Okay, okay," Clifford said. "Here. Ninety-nine dollars and ninety-nine cents."

"Well, that's better," Hannah said. "Still, I think Lian is worth more than ninety-nine dollars and ninety-nine cents."

"You know," Clifford said, handing Lian's mother a red envelope, "you are completely right. She is worth much more than ninety-nine dollars and ninety-nine cents. Here."

Hannah took the envelope from Lian's mother and started counting it. $200, $300, $500 . . . $999.99! Everyone exclaimed and shouted in appreciation. I didn't say anything because I was shocked. I didn't know Clifford was so rich. Maybe his grandparents gave him the money.

red envelope
stuffed with
$999.99

"Okay," Hannah said, "You can have your bride. Lian!"

And out came Lian. She looked even

prettier than she had at the church. She was sparkling red and gold and in the light she glittered like tinsel on a Christmas tree. Clifford grinned like a jack-o-lantern as he saw her.

"C'mon everyone," Clifford said as he offered Lian his arm, "Let's go and eat!"

Chapter 22

Double Happiness

tea pot and cups

I THOUGHT THAT AS SOON AS WE SAT DOWN IN the dining room we'd get food, but we didn't. Another gong clanged and everyone was quiet. Clifford's parents and Lian's mother and grandmother were sitting on chairs at the front of the room. Behind them on the wall was a big lobster-red sign with a Chinese symbol on it. Next to Clifford and Lian was a small table with a white teapot, polished and smooth. With two hands Lian offered a teacup to Clifford's father.

"What's happening?" I asked Mom.

"It's the tea ceremony," she told me. "See how Lian is serving tea to Clifford's parents? That's to symbolize that she is now part of his family. Clifford will do the same for Lian's mother and grandmother."

double happiness
symbol

"What does the sign say?" I asked.

"It means double happiness," Mom said. "Do you see how it is two characters that are exactly the same? Alone, that character means happiness. For weddings we repeat it, so it means double happiness. It's just like when two people are married; together they double their happiness."

Clifford and Lian finished serving the tea and kissed. And everyone cheered and clapped again. I guess that meant they were married again and that double happiness also meant double wedding ceremonies – American and Taiwanese.

And then, finally, the food! I was glad because I was hungry. We ate and ate. There were nine courses! I guess the nine meant forever with food, too, because it kept coming and coming. After the bird's nest soup (which wasn't made from a real bird's nest, just noodles that looked like a nest), each

the tea ceremony

116

the wedding banquet

table got a whole roasted chicken, lobster in a white sauce, a whole steamed fish, and a big platter of fried rice. There were also stir-fried vegetables with crunchy water chestnuts, crispy brown peking duck, and glossy red sweet and sour pork.

"Did you know that this food has a special meaning?" Dad said.

"Like on Chinese New Year," Lissy said, "like fish and dumplings mean money?"

"Yes," Dad said, "But here the chicken symbolizes the phoenix—which is the bride, and the lobster represents the dragon—which is the groom. So having them served for dinner means the couple is now together."

bouquet

I thought that was strange. We were eating the chicken and the lobster! Did that mean we were eating Lian and Clifford? By the time the cake was cut and the lotus-seed buns were served for dessert, I was so full I could hardly move. But when I heard Lian was throwing her bouquet, I jumped up. The wedding was almost over, and catching the bouquet was my last chance to be a part of it. Besides, I wanted the flowers.

But Lian threw it too high and Cousin Hannah leaped up and grabbed it in the air. No fair! But Mom said that whoever caught the bouquet was supposed to get married next, and I was too young to get married for a long time. So, maybe not getting the bouquet was, like Dad said, fate.

And that was the end of the wedding. We went back to the hotel. The sky was dark ink-blue and Dad carried Ki-Ki, who was half asleep. I felt sad—Clifford was married, the wedding was over, and I hadn't done anything for it except watch.

One Last Thing

Clifford and Lian
at the door

BUT JUST AFTER I FINISHED PUTTING ON MY FUZZY pajamas, there was a knock on the hotel room door. Mom opened it and there were Clifford and Lian!

"We need to borrow your kids," Clifford said. "Especially Pacy."

"Why?" I asked as we followed them out the door into the elevator. "What do you need me for?"

"We need you to jump on our bed," Clifford said. We all laughed. It was such a funny thing to ask me to do.

"We need all you kids to jump on the bed before we sleep on it," Lian said, "so that hopefully, some-day, we'll have kids, too."

"And I remembered when I had to climb through a

window a long time ago," Clifford said, "so I knew Pacy would be especially perfect for the job."

"What do you mean 'climb through a window'?" I asked. I had no idea what Clifford was talking about.

WHY CLIFFORD CLIMBED THROUGH A WINDOW

When you were just born, Lissy was very jealous of you. She was used to being the only one and getting all the attention, and when you came along she felt like everyone ignored her. She didn't like you at all.

One day, when I was about fifteen or sixteen years old, all of our families got together at my house. You probably still weren't even a year old yet, so while all the parents were talking you fell asleep. We didn't have a crib in our house, so your mom put you in my parents' bedroom upstairs.

But about five minutes later, we heard you crying. Your mom went upstairs to get you, but when she got to the room the door was closed and locked! Quickly, she called everyone upstairs to help.

We all crowded around the door to see if we could open it. We heard you crying and crying. And we heard something else. We heard giggling. It was Lissy! She was inside the room with you, laughing.

"Lissy," we called to her, "open the door! What's going on in there?"

But Lissy wouldn't open the door. She just kept laughing and you just kept crying. And none of us knew what was happening.

Finally my dad turned to me and said, "Clifford, we left the window open. Why don't you climb the tree outside and see if you can get into the room?"

So, I went outside and climbed the maple tree next to the house. When I finally reached the window I looked in the room, and you know what I saw? I saw Lissy jiggling the bed so you'd bounce. Every time she jiggled, you'd cry. And the louder you cried, the louder she laughed."

Lissy bouncing me (as a baby) with Clifford watching through the window

"Of course," Clifford ended, as we entered their hotel room, "I got in the room and rescued you. I was the hero; it was one of the most memorable days of my life."

"I got in a lot of trouble," Lissy said. "I remember, too."

I looked at Lissy. She didn't seem a bit sorry. "I guess I was lucky, back then," I said.

"Yes, you were," Clifford said. "And, since you were so lucky to be saved by me from that bouncing bed back then, I thought you could pay me back with some lucky bed jumping now."

"Okay!" I said as we leaped on top of their red silk-covered bed. My feet sank into the mattress and silk twisted around my ankles, but I didn't care. Finally I was part of the wedding! I jumped as hard as I could. One great jump almost bounced me off the bed, but Clifford caught me.

"Thanks," he said, smiling. "We couldn't have finished the wedding without you."

jumping on the bed for good luck

Chapter 24

Back to School

new socks
and shoes

ALL TOO SOON, LIKE A CHERRY POPSICLE ON A hot day, the summer melted away. It seemed like as soon as we got back from Clifford's wedding, Mom was driving us all to the mall to get new backpacks, socks, and shoes for our first day of school.

At school, my new teacher was Mr. Davidson. It was the first time I ever had a male teacher. He was tall, with glasses and brown hair the color of toasted bread. He was different from all the other teachers I'd had.

First, he was really picky. Everything we wrote had to be in cursive writing; we were too old to print things anymore, he told us. Also, all our papers had to be done the same way—the holes had to be on the left side, our names on the first blue line on top

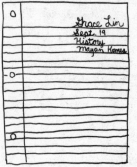

the way I labeled my papers
for Mr. Davidson

on the right-hand side, and the date, subject, and assignment lined up underneath.

But he also was fun, too. He let us choose our own seats, wherever we wanted. Becky, Charlotte, and I put our desks right next to each other, though I really wanted to sit next to Sam Mercer. And almost at the beginning of the year, he told us that our grade was going to have a talent show.

That was exciting! Everyone talked about what they wanted to do. For the first time, I wished my talent was something other than writing and drawing. You couldn't do that for a talent show.

"Becky and I want to do a dance to that song 'Love Me Forever,'" Charlotte told me. "Do you want to be in it too?"

I thought about it. Becky and Charlotte took dance lessons every Saturday and I wouldn't be able to do all the steps they did. Also, I didn't like that song "Love Me Forever," and I knew I'd feel really silly dancing in front of people to it.

"I don't know if I can dance like you guys," I said.

"Maybe I should think of doing something else."

"Kurt and Rich are going to lip synch a song," Becky told me. "They wanted to do the song 'I'm Too Sexy,' but Mr. Davidson told them to choose a different song."

"I know what you can do!" Charlotte said. "You and Dumb-Way can do a karate skit together. It can be like a scene from that kung fu movie. Hi-yaa!"

Suddenly, I felt like a blowfish puffed up in my throat. I hadn't seen Dun-Wei in a long time, even though I knew Mom talked to his mother on the phone a lot. It wasn't that I had forgotten about him, it was just that I tried not to think about him, as much

Charlotte doing pretend karate

as possible. Whenever I did, I always felt uncomfortable. It was easier just to put him out of my mind. And, usually, since he was in Mrs. Janey's class, that wasn't too hard.

But everyone still seemed to pair us up. Now Charlotte was even saying Dun-Wei and I should be in the talent show together!

"I don't even know karate," I said. As I watched

Charlotte try to do pretend karate, the annoyed feeling I had when I was with them came back, like a black fly that I couldn't swat.

"Oh, well," Becky said. "If you can't think of anything, you can join our dance."

"Maybe," I said. I didn't know what to do. I still felt worried and confused. It seemed like this new school year was going to be exactly the same as last year.

Chapter 25

Wishes

moon cakes

EVEN THOUGH I AVOIDED DUN-WEI AS MUCH AS possible, I couldn't always escape. Mom and Dun-Wei's mother were now good friends. Such good friends that in October they decided that we should celebrate the Moon Festival together. We were all going to go to the park, have a night picnic, and watch the moon. The Pans, the Taiwanese family that lived an hour away from us, were coming, too. They had some relatives who had come to visit and two boys, Teddy and Phil, as well as a girl named Emily, were coming as well.

We had never celebrated the Moon Festival before, even though Mom and Dad had talked about it.

roasting
chestnuts on
the grill

Mom said it was kind of like a Chinese Thanksgiving—a time where families cele-brated being together, but you ate moon cakes instead of turkey.

It was already dark when we left, so as soon as we got to the park all the kids helped the adults make a charcoal fire in the grill. Once the fire was crackling and burning orange, Dun-Wei's mom put a pan of chestnuts over it. Mom and Mrs. Pan were laying out the platters of cold chicken, noodles, rice, and a big bowl of soup, still warm from home. Teddy started to poke in the box where the golden-baked moon cakes were, but his mom shooed him away.

"Those are for later," she told him. "Save them for when the moon comes out and you make your wish. Have some soup instead."

"We wish when the moon comes out?" Lissy asked, as we each took a bowl of soup.

"Yes," Dad told us. "When the moon is at its fullest,

you can tell the moon your most secret wish. You don't say it out loud; you just think of what your heart wants the most and the moon will hear it."

"And does it come true?" I asked.

"Sometimes," Dad said. "It depends on the moon."

"Sometimes it depends on yourself," Mom told me. "Remember what we talked about at Chinese New Year, about resolutions and wishes? Sometimes you can make your wishes come true by resolving to do things."

"But for all the other things," Dad said, "you can ask the moon."

I was excited about my wish. I felt like I had wasted my birthday wish, so this looked like a second chance. As I thought about what I'd wish for, I put a spoonful of soup in my mouth. Yuck! I made a face. It didn't taste good. The soup left a dry, sharp taste in my mouth, like it had been made of rubber bands. I pushed the bowl away from my plate.

"The kids don't like the soup." Dun-Wei's mother laughed. I looked and saw that Lissy, Ki-Ki, Teddy, and

bitter melon soup

Phil had pushed their soup away, too.

"Ah, it's because it's bitter-melon soup," Dad said, "and they are young. You can only appreciate bitter-melon soup when you are old and have tasted the bitterness of life."

I thought about that. With Melody moving, my bad grade in school, my worries about the cold door, and all the other changes during the Year of the Rat, I felt like I had tasted the bitterness of life. I should be able to eat the soup. Carefully, I took another spoonful. Yuck! Nope, I still didn't like it.

But, then, I looked up again and saw Dun-Wei eat-

Dun-Wei's mother with lanterns

ing it. He was the only one who liked it. He kept putting spoonfuls into his mouth and swallowing.

And suddenly I began to think about the bitterness he had tasted. Ever since Melody left, I had felt alone in school. I realized that he probably felt the same way, only a hundred times worse. He probably hated that he was fresh off the boat. He probably wished he had never come to upstate New York, to the school where kids made fun of him and I thought he was the enemy and ignored him. And suddenly, I felt guilty.

Mrs. Liu came over with round paper lanterns. Dun-Wei handed me a softly lit circle.

"Thanks," I said.

"Bu ke qi," Dun-Wei said. Then he stopped and smiled and said, "I mean, you're welcome."

As he moved away, I clutched my lantern. It was as if the soft light was making me see clearly at last. Because I finally saw that all this time I had been calling Dun-Wei the enemy when I was a traitor. I turned my back on him because he was Chinese; and that was horrible because I was kind of Chinese, too.

So when the moon filled the sky like a mango-colored pearl, I was surprised at my

making my
secret wish

secret wish. I didn't wish for Melody to come back or for Sam Mercer to like me or for me to become an author and an illustrator. I didn't even wish for the changes of the Year of the Rat to go away. Instead I found myself wishing that I, too, could change.

Chapter 26

Fall

fall leaves

THE LEAVES ON THE TREES SEEMED TO WANT TO give one last glorious burst of color before falling to the ground like brown-colored ashes. Mom and Dad were the same way; they both had things they wanted to do before winter came. Dad wanted to play golf and Mom wanted to fix our house.

Dad was golf crazy. He played golf with Dr. Pan, who was Sandy Pan's father. He lived an hour away from New Hartford, but Dad drove thirty minutes one way to the golf

Dad playing golf in the cold

course and Dr. Pan drove thirty minutes the other way. The fall weather didn't discourage him, either. If frost covered the ground, Dad just layered on an extra jacket and hat. And every day, he hit golf balls in our backyard, practicing his swing. Mom would find golf balls in her garden, like a new kind of flower seed.

Mom wanted to make changes to our house. She especially thought we needed to change our carpets. I kind of agreed with her. Our carpet was supposed to be white, but now it was the beige color of a brown egg.

"I don't know," Dad said, unconvinced. "Do we really want to change the carpet? I think I'm too busy."

"Too busy playing golf," Lissy snorted.

Dad laughed. "Yes," he agreed, "too busy playing golf. I still haven't beaten Dr. Pan."

"Dr. Pan always beats you," Ki-Ki said.

"I know, I know," Dad said. "I think it's my putting. If I could just hit the ball in a straight line, I could beat him."

"Wait, we're not talking about golf," Mom said, interrupting. "What about the carpet?"

The side of Dad's face squished down in a grumpy

grimace as he thought. But in the next instant, Dad's eyes lit up, transformed. "You want to change the carpet?" he asked. "Even the hallway carpet upstairs?"

"Yes," Mom said. "It all has to be changed."

"Okay," Dad said. "That's fine. You can change the house any way you want."

We were all surprised. Dad usually didn't change his mind that fast. But Mom was so glad he was convinced that she didn't ask any questions. "Good," she said. "I'll call the carpet company tomorrow."

That night, after dinner, while I was trying to write a new story, Daddy called me.

"Pacy," Dad called from the hallway, "I need one of your art markers."

Dad draws a line down
the hallway

"Why?" I asked as I brought them to him.

"Oh, I just need one," he said as he picked out a red one. Then he started laying out a measuring tape.

"What are you doing?" Lissy asked as she came up the stairs.

"Here, you can help," Dad said, handing her the end of the tape. She stretched the measuring tape down the long hallway.

"Is it straight?" he asked us. We helped him make sure it wasn't crooked. Lissy held one end and I held the other. Then Dad took the red marker and drew a red line down the whole hallway, right on the carpet! He followed the measuring tape, so the line was exactly straight.

"Good!" he said. "Now I can practice my putting." And he did. He took his golf ball and tried to hit it so it followed the line.

When Mom saw the red line in the hallway, she was so shocked. Lissy and I laughed and laughed.

"No wonder you said it was okay to change the carpet," Mom said. "You just wanted an excuse so it would be okay for you to draw on it."

Mom scheduled for the carpet man to come and

change the carpet the next week. That gave Dad a whole week to practice his putting in the hallway. We helped him watch the golf ball roll down the red line. Every day, Dad hit the ball straighter and straighter.

When the carpet man came, we watched him pull out the old carpet. It made a *RR-rrr-iii-p!* sound. "Good-bye, red line!" Ki-Ki said. We felt bad for Dad; he was going to be sad when he came home.

But we were wrong. Dad came home very happy.

"Guess what?" he said. "I beat Dr. Pan today!"

Chapter 27

Our huo guo
Thanksgiving dinner

IT WAS ALREADY NOVEMBER, BUT IT STILL HADN'T snowed. I wished it would; outside everything was gray and brown like a dirty oyster shell. The wind blew as if it were trying to sweep the dead leaves away, but all it did was scatter them, and the ground was covered with crumbled leaves. But at least we had a couple of days of school off. It was Thanksgiving!

This year for dinner we had *huo guo*. Instead of rice, we cracked a raw egg in our bowls and mixed it with soy sauce. In a hot pot in the middle of the table, moon-colored broth simmered. All around it were plates of thinly sliced raw meat, shrimps, scallops, and vegetables that we would cook in the hot pot, dip in our raw egg to cool, then eat. It was always fun to eat huo guo. Everyone would get confused about whose food was whose because it was hard to keep track of what was cooking. "Where's my shrimp?" Dad would ask. "Did it swim away?"

There was also a small cooked turkey on the table too. That's because it was Thanksgiving and you have to have turkey on Thanksgiving! We never let Mom forget the turkey, though she tried to.

"You know Dad and I don't like turkey," Mom said. She said this every year. "You're going to have to eat it all. It's just going to be your lunch until it's all gone."

turkey sandwich

But we didn't care, because we knew it wasn't a Thanksgiving dinner without turkey. No matter what else there was when we sat down at the table for dinner, the turkey made it Thanksgiving. At least we thought so.

"Mrs. Lafontaine said that at Thanksgiving we should say what we are thankful for. I said I was thankful for our family and that I have a loose tooth," Ki-Ki said as we were eating. Mrs. Lafontaine was Ki-Ki's teacher, and Ki-Ki loved her. Ever since school began, a lot of Ki-Ki's sentences started, "Mrs. Lafontaine says . . ."

"That's a good way to celebrate the holiday," Mom said. "Let's say what we are thankful for. I am thankful for everyone's good health, our good food, and our nice house. Who's next?"

"Hmm, you took all of mine," Dad said. "I'm thankful that I don't have to work today and . . ."

"And you beat Dr. Pan in golf," I added.

"Yes, that, too," Dad agreed. "Okay, Lissy, how about you?"

Lissy made a face. "I'm thankful that we don't have school tomorrow," Lissy said.

My turn. This was annoying. What did I have to be thankful for? Melody was gone, I wasn't sure if I was really friends with Becky and Charlotte, I was ashamed of how I acted toward Dun-Wei, and my talent was a cold door that I couldn't even use in the talent show.

"I don't have anything to be thankful for," I said.

"Of course you do," Mom said. "Think."

"Okay," I said. "I'm thankful that I'm going to have a turkey sandwich on Monday."

"You're not really thankful for that," Lissy said. "Liar."

"Well," Mom said, "you should be thankful for that. Did I ever tell you the story about my school lunch?"

MOM'S SCHOOL LUNCH

When I was in school, we didn't bring our lunch in a paper bag or buy it from a school cafeteria. We carried it in a bamboo box. And when we entered our classroom, we all placed our boxes in a large mesh bag, like a fishnet, by the door. At lunchtime, one of the teachers would take the bag of lunches and put it in a giant steamer in another room. And when she brought it back to us, our lunches were so hot that I was afraid they would leave burn marks on our desks.

Nobody really liked their lunch food after it had been reheated. No matter how delicious the food was when it was packed, the steamer made everything tasteless. And it gave the pork dumplings, sticky rice, or soy sauce eggs a strange texture, kind of like melted wax.

A few of the luckier and richer students in my class had a hot lunch delivered to them at

bag of lunch boxes

141

lunchtime. Old grandmothers or aunts or sometimes servants would come at lunchtime and hand the student his or her lunch, bowing to the teacher the whole time. I begged and whined to my mother to do the same thing, but she just shook her head.

There was one girl in my class who got her lunch delivered to her every day. Her name was Chan and her older brother brought her box in promptly at noon. I didn't like her, and it wasn't just because I was jealous that she got a fresh lunch every day. It was because she never shared it.

Chan eating her lunch

Whenever Chan got her lunch from her brother, she would go to the far corner of the room and secretly eat. She'd hold the lid so it would block her food and mouth from view, but we could see her chewing and swallowing. And whenever someone came over, she'd quickly cover it. While the rest of us would divide our cement-gray pork dumplings and rubbery buns, she just sat alone in the corner. Her lunch was probably really good; probably sweet, meaty pink and white lobster or tea-smoked duck with crispy skin, and she wanted to eat it all herself. I thought she was mean and selfish.

One day, my mother told me that since she had an errand to run near the school, and because she was tired of hearing me complain, she would bring me a fresh hot lunch. I was so excited. The whole morning I had a hard time paying attention to the lessons because I was so eager for my mother to come with my lunch.

To my dismay, our lessons were running late. When noon came, my teacher was still talking, so when my mother and the other fresh lunches came they had to pile them in a corner on the desk. I was so worried. Was my fresh lunch going to get cold? Would the teacher say we had to reheat them? I hoped not! That would be horrible—the one time I got a fresh lunch and it might be ruined!

So when the teacher finally called time for lunch, I rushed to the desk and grabbed my box. At least I thought it was my box. It felt very light, like a paper balloon. I opened it and was shocked. The lunch box was empty!

"That's my lunch box," I heard a voice say. I looked up and saw Chan. She quickly grabbed it and covered it so no one could see. Her eyes were large like a scared rabbit as she looked at me. "Don't tell anyone, okay?" she whispered.

During the rest of lunchtime, she told me how her family was too poor to give her lunch. Chan and her

empty lunch box

brother didn't want everyone to know how poor they were so they had saved their pennies to buy the lunch box. And every day, in his high school, he pretended to eat lunch from it and then afterward, brought it to her, so she could pretend to eat, too. She begged me not to tell anyone.

I had been completely wrong about Chan. All this time, I thought she was the lucky one, with fresh lunches full of rich food, while she had really been eating shadows from a shared lunch box. That afternoon, I divided my wrapped sticky rice in half and shared it with her. After that, I shared my lunch with her every day, and I never told anyone about Chan's empty lunch box.

"Until now," Lissy said.

"Yes," Mom said, "but that was a long time ago, so I think it's okay. Anyway, the point is that I should've been thankful that I had any lunch—fresh or not. Just like you should be thankful that you get a lunch, even if it is a turkey sandwich."

I stirred my sliced meat in the hot broth and as it turned brown, I thought about Mom's story. Maybe Mom was right. There were always things to be thankful for and I was just looking at things wrong. Maybe, instead of wishing Melody hadn't left, I should just be glad that she had been here and that Charlotte and Becky still were. And, even if I couldn't use my talent for the talent show, at least I had a talent. Maybe I should be thankful for all the bad things because they could be even worse. But if that was true, that meant what I should really be thankful for was that I was me, which seemed strange because of all of my mistakes and worries.

Somehow, it seemed a lot easier to be thankful for a turkey sandwich.

Chapter 28

Sam Mercer and the Black Spiders

BACK AT SCHOOL, IT SEEMED LIKE EVERYONE WAS busy with the talent show except for me. I knew that wasn't really true; there were lots of people who didn't get in or didn't try out, like me. But it seemed like every day, people were practicing or rehearsing while I just watched.

Most people were singing or dancing or lip synching songs. Even Dun-Wei was in the talent show. Sam Mercer found out that Dun-Wei could play the piano and got him to play keyboards for his band, the Black Spiders. I had thought about singing or playing the violin or joining Becky and Charlotte in their dance of cartwheels and kicks, but in the end I didn't. None of those things were what I wanted to do.

The truth was that I already knew what my talent was. It was writing and drawing books. I remembered Mom's story and tried to be thankful for my talent, but it was hard. Not only was my talent wrong for the talent show, it was a cold door. I used to think my talent was so great, but now I was starting to change my mind.

"For the talent show," Mr. Davidson said, "we've decided that someone in our class will do the poster, while someone in Mrs. Janey's class will create the programs. So, who would like to design the poster?"

volunteering to make the Talent Show poster

A poster! Even though it wasn't making a book, I had the talent to do that. I raised my arm so fast it was as if it were being pulled by a string. Mr. Davidson smiled.

"Well," Mr. Davidson said, "I think our resident artist wants the job. Okay, Grace, after class I'll give you the poster board and you can bring it home to work on it."

The poster board was big. It came up to my shoulders and I had to place it on the top of my toes when

I carried it so I didn't kick it. Since this was the only way I was going to be able to show my talent at the talent show, I wanted to do a good job. I remembered how for our quilt-square project we had to do practice drawings, so I did a couple of rough drafts first. I was glad I did. Mr. Davidson told me the poster had to have the words "Oxford Rd. Elementary School Talent Show" as well as the date and time, and it was hard to fit everything in.

I put "Oxford Rd. Elementary School Talent Show" in a box in the middle and the date and time on the bottom. And then all around the border I drew pictures of some of the acts in the talent show. I drew Becky and Charlotte dancing, Sam Mercer's band,

making the poster

the Black Spiders (I drew them the biggest), Holly Honchell singing, even Kurt and Rich lip synching. I used all the colors in my marker set. I used my black marker so much that it dried up and I had to get another one. It took me a long time; so long that I didn't bring it to school until the night of the talent show.

But when I brought it to school, no one paid attention to me. Everyone was rushing around putting makeup on, going over music, or tying dance shoes. When I brought the poster to Mr. Davidson, all he said was, "Oh, good, the poster." And quickly, without even looking, he hung it up on the wall right next to the door of the auditorium and ran to check the sound equipment for the microphones.

I was starting to feel like a popped balloon. As the audience started to go into the auditorium, most of them didn't even look at my poster. The ones that did only glanced at it and kept walking. It was so unfair. No one cared about my talent at all.

I guessed it was because the talent show was showing the real talent. Becky and Charlotte did their dance and got a standing ovation, Sam Mercer's band made the walls shake (and some parents cover

Charlotte and Becky's
dance

their ears), and Kurt and Rich's lip synching made the crowd shout with laughter. These talents were the important ones, the ones people liked and cared about. My talent was just a cold wind on a winter day.

So after the final clapping, while the lights went up and the crowds outside the auditorium were congratulating and photographing all the performers, I carefully took down my poster and carried it home. No one was looking at it anyway.

Chapter 29

Famous

newspaper

THE NEXT MORNING AT BREAKFAST, DAD SLAPPED the newspaper in front of my bowl of rice porridge.

"You're a star!" he said. "Can I have your autograph?"

What was he talking about? And then I saw it. There was a picture of me in the paper! I couldn't believe it! It was a picture of me carrying my poster. The title of the photo said, "Oxford Rd. Elementary Shows Many Talents," and underneath it the caption said, "The Oxford Rd. Elementary School held its Talent Show last night. The singing, dancing, and music talents of the school were captured in the poster by the drawing talent of Grace Lin."

The big poster almost covered me completely;

Oxford Rd. Elementary Shows Many Talents

The Oxford Rd. Elementary School held its Talent Show last night. The singing, dancing, and music talents of the school were captured thanks to the drawing talent of Grace Lin, who created this poster.

my photo in the newspaper

you could just see my head and the top part of my shoulder. I didn't know they took my picture! I wasn't looking at the camera, so they must have taken it when I was looking away. Suddenly, the world that had seemed so gloomy was sparkling like ginger ale in a glass cup. I'd never had my photo in the paper before. My poster was in there and they wrote about MY talent. Someone had paid attention after all.

"Can I cut the picture out to bring to school?" I asked. I couldn't wait to show everyone.

But when I got to school, everyone already knew. I

was famous! Becky had cut it out of her newspaper to show me just in case I hadn't seen it. Mr. Davidson hung a copy from his newspaper on the door of his classroom and Mrs. Janey hung one on her door. The whole class gathered around

famous at school

and tried to see whom I had drawn on the poster. It was a little hard to tell since the photo was a lot smaller than the real thing, so Mr. Davidson asked if I could bring the poster back in again. Sam Mercer even asked me if I could draw a poster for his band!

I had been wrong to change my mind about my talent. It was a pretty good one to have. I don't know why I had ever doubted it.

Chapter 30

Resolutions

Snow *

THE WEATHER SEEMED TO TURN COLD IN A SNAP. Even though we thought we were ready, everyone was surprised when snow fell from the sky as if someone were pouring down sugar.

"Lots of snow today!" Dad said in the morning. "You lucky kids! The radio said that there's no school. It's so cold outside that it's breaking records. I wish I could have a snow day. I'm going to turn into a snowman going to work today." No school! It was like a surprise vacation. I was all ready to go outside and play until I

opening the cold door

opened the door. BRRR! The cold wind bit my face, and the inside of my nose stung as if icicles suddenly formed there. I closed the door.

"It's so cold out there!" I said, shivering. "It froze my nose!"

Dad laughed and said, "I warned you. That's what you get when you open a cold door!"

All of a sudden, Dad saying that reminded me about the other cold door—the cold door of becoming an author and illustrator. Even though I didn't have any doubts about my talent anymore, I still didn't like that door. But for almost two years, I had thought that being an author and illustrator was what I wanted to be and who I was going to become. Now, I just didn't know. Was being an author and illustrator just a wishful dream or was it something I could make happen? Was it even something I should try to make happen?

"Remember at Chinese New Year when we wrote resolutions?" I asked Dad. "Remember how you told me some things you made happen and other things you just wished?"

Dad nodded.

"Well, how do you know which is which?" I asked. "And how do you know which are the things you should try for?"

"Well, this is a hard question for so early in the morning," Dad said. "Hmm, I guess it's different for every person. You have to know yourself what you can do."

"Can't someone just tell me?" I said. "It's too hard to figure it out."

"No, no one can tell you," Dad said. "Only you can decide, because only you know who you are."

"You know who I am," I said. "And Mom, too. You're my parents."

"We are your parents," Dad said. "But that doesn't mean we truly know you. It's like that little story . . ."

KNOWING THE FISH

One day two philosophers were walking outdoors. As they crossed a bridge, they stopped and saw an orange fish glide through the muddy green water, like floating tangerine peels. In the sunlight, the fish sparkled like fireflies.

fish

"The fish are happy today," one philosopher said to the other.

"How do you know?" the other

two philosophers looking
at the fish

philosopher replied. "You're not a fish."

"The friends continued walking. Their footsteps crunched the carpet of golden leaves as they passed, and each was quiet. The first philosopher was deep in thought, considering their conversation.

Finally he said to the other, "How do you know that I don't know that the fish are happy?" the first philosopher said. "You are not me."

"So, you see," Dad said, "only you really know yourself and only you can really make your decisions."

And I guessed Dad was right. It was up to me. All the things I didn't like—being scared of the cold door, feeling ashamed about Dun-Wei and being Chinese, getting bad grades, feeling weird with Becky and Charlotte, even trying to get Sam Mercer to notice me—I was the one who had to change those things. And knowing that was a little scary. "Why do you look so frightened all of a sudden?" Dad asked.

"I didn't realize I'd have to decide and do things," I said. "I liked it better when you and Mom did everything."

"Ah, you're growing up," Dad said. "Don't worry, it's not that bad. Do you remember how I told you the story about the twelve animals of Chinese New Year? The tiger came in third place, without a raft or friends helping him. He looked at the wild and fierce waters and went in, relying on just himself, his courage and strength to get across. You were born in the year of the tiger, so you're brave. You can face anything."

Dad's words warmed me as if I had put on a fur coat. I could be brave. I didn't need tiger luck; I was a tiger. I could almost feel the tiger stripes on my back. I wouldn't let the changes of the Year of the Rat sink me.

Chapter 31

Brave like a Tiger

talking to Melody

THAT NIGHT, MELODY WAS SO EXCITED WHEN SHE called me I could barely understand what she was saying.

"Guess what?" she said. "Guess what? I'm coming back to New Hartford to visit!"

I couldn't believe it, but it was true. Melody was going to come back to visit. Her parents were selling the house to Dun-Wei's family, and Melody's mom had to come back and take care of some paperwork and details. Melody's mom asked if she could stay with us while she was here, and she was going to bring Melody because "We know you two would never forgive us if I came alone."

But they weren't coming until around Chinese New

Year. That seemed SO far away. But, luckily, the winter days were blowing by. In school we were doing open projects again, about endangered animals. And this time, I was making a book.

"Are you sure you don't want to be a third partner?" Becky asked out on the playground at recess. We were watching the boys play football in the snow. The boys liked to play football in the snow because then they could dive on the ground without getting hurt. We liked to watch because it was funny to see them covered in snow—especially Sam Mercer, who rolled around so much that he looked like a gingerbread cookie with white icing. "You'll have to do all that work on panda bears by yourself," Becky added.

boys playing
football in the snow

"That's okay," I said. "If I want to be an author and illustrator, I better practice as much as I can."

"What if you don't become an author and illustrator?" Charlotte asked. "Then you would have done all that practicing for nothing."

"It won't be for nothing," I said, trying to feel as brave as a tiger. "I know I'm going to be one, no matter what."

And after I said that, I did feel like a brave tiger. What did I care about cold doors when I had fur that was thick and warm? Just like the tiger that jumped into the wild water because he wanted to win the race, I was going jump through the door and become an author and illustrator. I wouldn't be afraid anymore.

"So, when is Melody coming back?" Charlotte asked. I had told them all about her phone call that morning.

"In a couple of months," I said, smiling. "Just in time for Chinese New Year."

"Well, maybe it's good you're doing the project by yourself, then," Becky said in a funny voice. "We won't see you at all once Melody arrives."

I stopped smiling. Suddenly I understood why everything felt clumsy and awkward when I was with

Charlotte and Becky. When Melody had moved here two years ago, we had become best friends, and I had stopped being such good friends with Becky and Charlotte. Not only had I ignored them and probably hurt their feelings, all the things that I had been interested in and cared about were different now. They hadn't changed. I had changed.

"Wow, look at that throw!" Charlotte said as a ball whizzed through the air. "Who threw that?"

"It was Dumb-Way!" Becky said. "Can you believe it? I guess Dumb-Way is a pretty good football player."

I took a deep breath and gathered my tiger strength. If I was ever going to make things better with Becky and Charlotte, I'd have let them know how I had changed. I had to let them know that the things that wouldn't have bothered me before, bothered me now.

"I don't think it's nice to call him Dumb-Way," I said. "His name is Dun-Wei."

"But everyone calls him that," Becky said.

I swallowed hard and looked at my feet. "I don't," I said, "because I think it's kind of mean."

When I peeked up, I saw Becky looking at me with her head cocked like a surprised pigeon. Slowly, she nodded. "You're right," she said. "It is mean. I won't do it anymore."

"Thanks," I said, and it was as if the ice in my stomach had suddenly melted away. "You know what? When Melody comes, you two should come over. I bet my mom would let me have a sleepover."

"Yeah, that'd be fun!" Charlotte said and they smiled at me.

I smiled back. Everything would be all right. Deep inside of me, I heard a tiger roar. It was so loud and strong I was surprised. I never knew it was there before.

tiger
roar

Chapter 32

Kaufmann's holiday store window

ONE OF THE GOOD THINGS ABOUT WINTER WAS that there were so many vacations. After Thanksgiving, we had Christmas and New Year's off and then another vacation in February. I was really looking forward to the one in February because that's when Melody was coming. But now, it was Christmas and even though it wasn't the vacation I most wanted to happen, I still had a good time.

For Christmas, Mom took us shopping for our presents. We didn't give presents the way most American families did, where they bought things ahead of time and wrapped them up for a surprise. Mom just took us shopping and bought us what we wanted. She said Chinese people usually just gave people money, anyway. This used to bother me, but now I thought this was the best way to do it. It was too easy for Mom to make a mistake otherwise.

Lissy didn't come shopping with us. She said she'd just take the money and get what she wanted herself. She never wanted to go shopping with us anymore, even though she went to the mall all the time. She didn't want her friends to see her with us. Mom said Lissy was going through "a phase."

Shopping was fun. All the stores glittered red and gold and green with their holiday decorations and Christmas carols jingled merrily through the loudspeakers. Ki-Ki and I liked to look at the outside window of the Kaufmann's department store. Every Christmas they put up a special holiday display. This year they had a toy Santa with his reindeer. Out of all the displays I could remember, it was my favorite, though they didn't have red-nosed Rudolph. I guess they forgot.

First we went to the toy store for Ki-Ki. They had hula hoops and plastic cars and dollhouses as tall as I was. Ki-Ki liked looking at all the Barbie dolls, though Mom would NEVER get her one. Barbie had long blond hair and shiny clothes, just like the princess in *Cinderella* or *Sleeping Beauty*. I kind of understood why Ki-Ki liked that doll; when I was younger, I thought Barbie was beautiful. But Mom didn't think so at all.

"You don't want one of those," Mom said to Ki-Ki.

"Please!" Ki-Ki said. "Everyone else has one! Only our family isn't allowed to have Barbie. It's not fair!"

That wasn't 100 percent true. Melody hadn't been allowed to have a Barbie doll either. I think our mothers talked to each other.

"It's her Christmas present," I said, trying to help Ki-Ki. "You promised you'd get us whatever we wanted."

Mom sighed. "Okay," she said, and she scanned down the aisle. Her eyes stopped at the "Dolls of the World Barbie." These were Barbie dolls dressed up to look like they were from different countries. They were more expensive than the regular ones, which were on sale, but Mom didn't seem to notice. Instead she picked up the Barbie from China with the dark red dress and black hair and offered it to Ki-Ki.

the Barbie Mom bought Ki-Ki

"How about this one?" Mom said.

Ki-Ki grabbed it. I think she was so

excited that Mom was actually going to buy her one, that she would've taken anything. "Okay!" she said.

"How about you, Pacy?" Mom asked.

We left the toy store because I felt like I was too old for toys, and we went to the book store. I knew Becky and Charlotte would think wanting books for a Christmas present was weird, but I didn't care. That was what I wanted.

"How many can I get?" I asked.

the books I chose for Christmas

"Hmm," Mom said. "How about three?"

"How come Pacy gets three books and I only get one doll?" Ki-ki asked. I knew she was hoping she could get another doll.

"You can get a book, too," Mom told her. Ki-Ki quickly grabbed a Barbie book. Mom wrinkled her nose, but let her have it.

I picked my three books out carefully. Finally I decided on *Anne of Green Gables*, *The Last Unicorn*, and *Theater Shoes*.

"Are you sure you want those?"

Mom asked. "Those seem a lot longer than the other books you read."

I nodded. I had picked them out especially because they were extra thick. I was hoping they would help make the days go by faster while I waited for February vacation, Chinese New Year, and Melody to come.

Chapter 33

Waiting for Melody

Our Christmas
tree at Chinese New Year

I KNEW CHINESE NEW YEAR WAS COMING WHEN
we finally threw out the Christmas tree. It was only
then that Dad was forced to stop putting off throwing
it out. In the meantime, the pine needles looked like
brown grains of rice and whenever anyone passed a
cascade fell to the floor.

Dad dragged the tree out to
the trash and Mom swept the
floors. She swept the needles
and every speck of dust out the
back door.

Mom
sweeps

"We have to sweep all the bad
luck out of the house now,"

Mom said. "The first day of the year is the broom's birthday."

"The broom has a birthday?" I asked, laughing. "Do we give it a party?"

"No," Mom said, "we give it a rest. No one is allowed to use a broom on the New Year. If you do, you'll sweep all your good luck and your money away."

"For real?" I asked; I was starting to think these superstitions were silly.

"Who knows?" Mom said. "But why risk it?"

That was true. So when Mom had us hang the red banner on our door, get our hair cut, and go through all the chopsticks to throw out any that had chipped (because that would mean something was eating away your fortune), we didn't complain. Though I felt like

red banners decorating
our door

Mom was being pickier about Chinese New Year than she usually was. She even bought new sheets

Looking at the catalog

and silk dresses for us. But I did like getting a new dress; I could finally stop wearing Lissy's old green one.

Mom said we could choose whatever we wanted for our new Chinese dresses. She ordered them from a catalog, so Lissy, Ki-Ki, and I lay on the ground looking at it, turning every glossy page and inspecting each picture carefully.

"I want the one that is all white," Ki-Ki said. Ever since she was a flower girl, she wanted all her clothes to be winter white.

"No, no," Mom said. "You can't wear a white Chinese dress. In Chinese tradition, white is the color of funerals."

"Really?" Lissy said. "What's black for then?"

"Well, people wear black for funerals, too," Mom

the dress I wanted

said. "Both of those colors are not lucky to wear for Chinese New Year."

Lissy looked disappointed. I knew she wanted to get a dress that was all black because she said black was always stylish. Instead she chose dark blue again.

"Don't get dark blue again," I told her. "What's the point of getting a new dress if it's almost exactly the same?"

"That's true," Mom said. "Especially since your old blue dress still fits you. Also, one of the reasons why we get new clothes for the new year is so that it confuses any evil spirits. We're hoping that in your new clothes, they won't know you."

Lissy made a face, but she chose a deep eggplant purple dress with fortune flowers on it. Ki-Ki chose a pale, icy blue dress with butterflies. I knew I wanted the coral red one with goldfish on it, but what Mom had said about spirits not knowing us in our new clothes was bothering me. I hadn't seen Melody in a long time. Maybe when she came during Chinese New Year, she wouldn't know me, either. That would be horrible! I hoped that wouldn't be the last change of the Year of the Rat.

Chapter 34

Finally Chinese New Year!

waiting for morning

MELODY WAS COMING ON THE EVE OF CHINESE New Year. Our school was on winter vacation then, so it was perfect for me. Her school had a different schedule, but her mom arranged for her to take some days off.

The night before she came, I couldn't sleep. I was so excited! I felt like a popcorn kernel about to pop. But I was a little worried, too. Maybe we had both changed so much that we wouldn't be such good friends anymore. On my bed, I could see the night turn into morning out my window—a streak of light was spreading across the grim sky, like milk just poured into tea. As soon as the last bit of grayness faded away, I jumped out of bed to get everyone up. We had to go pick up Melody at the airport!

Melody Arrives

We got to the airport early and waited and waited. Melody's plane was late and I had almost given up hope that she was coming, but then she popped through the gate doors. She saw me and gave me a wide grin, as big as a watermelon slice; relief rushed through me. Nothing had changed. Melody still knew me and I still knew her. And when we were together again it was like she had never left. She looked exactly the same, except she was shorter. "I'm not shorter," she said when I told her this. "You're taller!"

We talked so fast to each other that Mom thought we were speaking another language. I told Melody everything I had already told her over the phone again, and all the things I had saved up to tell her—how I got an A+ on my Giant Panda book, how Dun-Wei replaced Kurt as the quarterback for the

the poster I made
for Sam Mercer

school football team when Kurt skipped too many practices, and how Sam Mercer smiled at me at lunch and told me the poster I did for the Black Spiders band was "awesome." I even told her about how I had decided Dun-Wei wasn't the enemy, and how I wasn't afraid of the cold door anymore.

Melody told me how in California it was so warm that at Christmastime she wore a T-shirt; there were so many cute boys there, even Asian boys—especially a boy named Gregory Chen who had long black hair—and that at the supermarket you could choose the fish you wanted from the tank and the butcher would hit it with a club to kill it for you. Everything was completely fascinating. It seemed like another world.

We talked so much that I didn't help Mom at all with the Chinese New Year dinner. Mom said it was okay, that I hadn't seen Melody in such a long time that I could just spend time with her. Besides, Melody's mom was helping. Though she probably wasn't enjoying it. I could hear Mom frying lots of unhealthy food.

"Time to eat!" Mom called.

Giggling and laughing, Melody and I came down the stairs. Lissy finished setting the table while Ki-Ki carefully scooped rice into bowls. The scoops of white rice were so perfectly rounded from the spoon that they looked like snowballs. Melody's mom set down the big bowl of bird's nest soup on the

bowl of rice

table with the red-brown roasted duck, purple eggplant shining with brown sauce that looked like syrup, leafy broccoli, golden pan-fried fish, the glistening jade-green cabbage and steamed light pink dumplings. All the rich, fried aromas mixed together and I smelled the familiar scent of Chinese New Year.

"Ah, it's nice to be together again for Chinese New Year, isn't it?" Dad said as we all sat down at the table. "I think that's the most important lesson of the Nian monster."

"What monster?" I asked.

"The Nian monster," Dad said. "The whole reason why we celebrate Chinese New Year."

THE NIAN MONSTER

A long time ago, a fierce monster that could eat up an entire village in one swallow lived in the mountains. More ferocious and wild than any dragon or unicorn, he only woke and fed one time a year, on the lunar New Year. But the horror and destruction he caused were unimaginable. All year long the people lived in fear and dread.

So when the days got closer and closer to Nian's feeding time, people began to despair.

"There must be something we can do to save ourselves and stop the Nian monster," they said. But what? The Nian monster was so strong and so enormous, no one could fight it. It would be worse than ants attacking a dragon. And the Nian monster came silently in the night, without warning. It wouldn't matter if they had an army fighting for them; the village would be destroyed before anyone even knew it. It was hopeless.

But one day, a wise old man came to the village.

"I know how you can survive the Nian monster," he said. "It is afraid of light, the color red, and loud noises.

On the night it wakes, you must cover your homes in red banners, light red lanterns, play loud drums, and set off firecrackers. It will scare Nian away and you will live another cycle."

The people thanked the old man and did as he said. They hung brilliant red banners, the color of a cooked crab shell, over their door and windows. They lit so many lanterns that their village looked as if it were on fire. They pounded their drums as if they were dangerous beasts and their fireworks deafened even those miles away. But even as they did this, they were afraid. What if the old man was wrong? What if all this failed and the Nian destroyed them?

So as the sun burned away from the sky like a dying coal, all feared it would be their last night on earth. They ate their favorite foods and wore their best clothes. Arguments were forgiven and debts were paid. Friends and family gathered together to be with each other one last time.

But when the light of the sun cracked through the dark sky, there was a great rejoicing! The old man had been right. The Nian monster had come and gone, scared by the red banners and loud noises. All were alive and the village was saved!

From then on, the New Year was celebrated this way. On the night when the Nian monster was to come, homes were decorated with red banners, favorite foods were eaten, and friends and family gathered together.

surviving the
Nian

"And, that is why we call Chinese New Year 'Guo Nian,'" Dad finished. "It means 'Survive the year' or really, 'surviving the Nian monster.'"

"Well, Happy Guo Nian!" Melody said, giving me a look. "We survived the changes of the Year of the Rat!"

"I guess the Year of the Rat did bring some changes," Dad said. "But the important things, like family and true friends, never change."

I thought about that. The Year of the Rat had brought a lot of changes and worries—Melody moving, Dun-Wei coming, my talent, and the cold door. A lot of them I hadn't liked and had made me uncomfortable or nervous. But I had survived.

And, looking around the table at Mom, Dad, Melody, Melody's mom, Ki-Ki, and even Lissy, I realized what Dad said was true. The important things never changed. I felt like I finally understood what Dad meant when he talked about fate and destiny and wishes and resolutions. The love of my friends and family was my fate, but I had the power to change and shape my destiny.

"Gong Xi Gong Xi Xin Nian Hao!" Melody said as she clinked her glass with mine: "Wishing you a good new year!"

"Wishing ALL of us a good New Year!" I said. But I

didn't need the good wishes. I grinned at everyone around the table, confident and sure. I knew this next new year was going to be good; in fact, all the new years after this were going to be great. I'd make sure of it.

Around the table

Author's Note

When I first began to receive responses from my first novel (this book's predecessor), *The Year of the Dog*, I was overwhelmed. "*The Year of the Dog* is a story kind of like my life," one girl told me. "I tried to read it slow so it wouldn't end."

And as she said that, I realized I didn't want the story to end either.

Because characters in books become friends to me; it's as if they are real people with real lives. Would I have loved Anne from *Anne of Green Gables* as much if I had gotten to know her through only one book? Or even Laura from *Little House in the Big Woods*? In fact, I was devastated that there were only nine books. I wanted to know what else happened.

So I decided to continue the story. However, even though the cover of this book says it is by me, it is really a shared ownership. Of course, I wrote the words, the sentences, crafted the plot and the dialogue. But the soul of the story isn't mine alone. It belongs to a number of people—my mother, my father, my sisters, my teachers, and my friends.

One friend in particular, however, does more than just share the story with me. Melody has a real-life counterpart—Alvina Ling, my best friend from child-hood who grew up, got a job at a publishing company, and became my editor for this book (and *The Year of the Dog*).

The Year of the Rat is about change, resolution, destiny, and fate. Why did we tear Melody and Pacy apart, sending Melody to California and leaving Pacy alone? Because it really happened! Alvina moved to California and we lived on either coast of the United States for many years. Distance and time usually fade relationships, but we were determined to remain friends. Letters (and later e-mails) flew back and forth, until we were adults with careers in the same industry. And when I put pen to paper for my novel, it seemed to be destiny when Alvina was able to acquire it and become my editor. Somehow, we were fated to create these books and together tell "what else happened."

I hope you like it!

Best Wishes,

Behind the Story

One of the first questions readers ask me about *The Year of the Dog* and *The Year of the Rat* is "Are all those stories true?" Well, the answer to that is yes and no. Some things are completely true, some things are partly true, and some are completely made up.

So what parts are true? Here are some of them:

The Year of the Dog and *The Year of the Rat* are both set in New Hartford, NY, where I grew up.

This is the house in the book:

our house

This is the house I grew up in.

The family in the story is based on my family when I was growing up.

My Family

I had a mom, a dad, an older sister named Lissy, and a younger sister named Ki-Ki. My American name is Grace and my Chinese name is Pacy.

Lissy did tease me a lot when I was younger. We didn't have a photo of Lissy bouncing me on the bed to make me cry but here is one of her putting me in the garbage can (maybe I will put that in another book):

Ki-Ki had a pink Chinese dress that she wouldn't let Mom button the collar of, just like in *The Year of the Dog*:

Ki-Ki
in her
dress

I went as a black and blue cat for Halloween:

me as a black cat

And I had a best friend too.

Melody and me

But in real life, her name was NOT Melody. Her name is Alvina (she's the one on the left).

Alvina really did move to California, just like in *The Year of the Rat*, but we stayed good friends. She even grew up to be my bridesmaid when I got married, just like we planned (though I didn't marry Teddy).

wedding drawing

And we're still friends now! She grew up to be a children's book editor and is the editor for this book (and *The Year of the Dog*).

The stories that Mom tells in the books are true or at least based on true experiences.

My grandfather did struggle as a doctor when he first began his practice until he gained fame and goodwill when he saved the life of a poor peddler who ran away because he could not pay for his care.

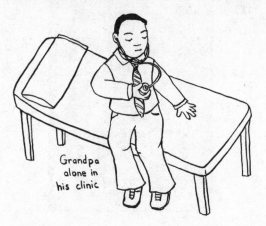

Grandpa
alone in
his clinic

My great-grandmother did walk my mother to school every morning and wait for her outside in the school-yard all day until school was out. My mother was so embarrassed that first day of school, until she saw all her classmates had their grandmothers waiting for them as well.

Mom (as a little girl) walking to school

When my mother grew older she really did grow roses on the roof of her building when she lived in Taiwan.

After she moved to the U.S., my great-grandmother took care of her garden.

And, just like in both books, I always did want to become an author and illustrator. This is the first book I ever made:

If you notice, I based Melody's book in *The Year of the Dog* on it:

Melody's Book

while my book:

my book

is based on the very first book of mine that was published:

because I really did grow up and become an author and illustrator of books!

So, those are some of the "real" things in my books. As you can see, they are full of true-life friendship, family, and dreams that have lasted through time, throughout cycles from the Year of the Rat to the Year of the Pig. No matter what each year brings—fortune, changes, new beginnings—they are what make my years lucky ones. And, hopefully, those are what will make yours lucky, too.

Best,
Grace Lin

Morgan Pace

Grace Lin

is the award-winning and bestselling author and illustrator of *The Year of the Dog*, *The Year of the Rat*, and *Dumpling Days*, as well as the Newbery Honor *Where the Mountain Meets the Moon*, *Starry River of the Sky*, and the National Book Award Finalist *When the Sea Turned to Silver*. Grace lives in Massachusetts, and invites you to visit her website at gracelin.com.

Laugh-out-loud with the lovable Pacy Lin!

SPECIAL EDITION PAPERBACKS!

Bonus content, deleted stories, Q&A's, and more in bestselling, award-winning author Grace Lin's modern classics.